Nathaniel Gee

SWEETWATER BOOKS
An imprint of Cedar Fort, Inc.
Springville, Utah

© 2022 Nathaniel Gee
All rights reserved.

No part of this book may be reproduced in any form whatsoever, whether by graphic, visual, electronic, film, microfilm, tape recording, or any other means, without prior written permission of the publisher, except in the case of brief passages embodied in critical reviews and articles.

This is a work of fiction. The characters, names, incidents, places, and dialogue are products of the author's imagination and are not to be construed as real. The opinions and views expressed herein belong solely to the author and do not necessarily represent the opinions or views of Cedar Fort, Inc. Permission for the use of sources, graphics, and photos is also solely the responsibility of the author.

ISBN 13: 978-1-4621-4276-7

Published by Sweetwater Books, an imprint of Cedar Fort, Inc.
2373 W. 700 S., Springville, UT 84663
Distributed by Cedar Fort, Inc., www.cedarfort.com

Library of Congress Control Number: 2022935675

Cover design by Shawnda T. Craig
Cover design © 2022 Cedar Fort, Inc.
Substantive by Rachel Hathcock
Edited and typeset by Valene Wood

Printed in the United States of America

10 9 8 7 6 5 4 3 2 1

Printed on acid-free paper

Dedicated to Merrill Kerr Gee II

*S*ociety has deemed that your ultimate measure as a parent comes down to your willingness to watch your children perform when no one else will. "True, I don't know my kids' names, but I never missed a basketball game." My father, by this standard, was a poor father. He rarely came to see me perform. My senior year I performed at every basketball and football game from out of bounds. I was a cheerleader. I do recall he came to one football game, and he was easy to spot among the fans. It wasn't because he was loudly cheering me on; rather, he was the only fan in the bleachers with a book in front of his face.

My father always had a book. He was an engineer by trade, but he loved to read everything from health books to the classics. This led to my brother being one of the few men on earth who can say they were named after Jane Austen. (Luckily they used the last name.) And while he wasn't at all my games, he was always there when I had a question. When I asked about economics, he introduced me to Leonard E. Reed. When I said I was bored, he introduced me to Sir Arthur Conan Doyle. And when I was bemoaning the rarity of true romantic humor, he introduced me to PG Wodehouse.

Anyone who reads my novels will readily see the impact PG Wodehouse has had on me. Without Wodehouse as a writer, there would be no author Nathaniel Gee. And while only a few would count this as one of his accomplishments, I am grateful for him, and more especially grateful to the world's greatest dad who introduced me to him.

Chapter 1

Celibacy

Celibacy. Perhaps no other word has as much power to thicken the blood, clam the palms, and cause general havoc on a man's insides. In 1557, it might have appeared that no job was as desirable as the clergy. The power, prestige, clerical immunity, and, of course, a steady income made it second only to royalty, which was not a bad gig, but a much harder career to break into at any point after birth. No, clergy was the pigs' stew, except for that one word, the snag, the fine print. Indeed, even for the most pious of men it was a hefty tradeoff: the benefits of the cloth for giving up . . . well, a lot. But, as is always the case, there are exceptions. And in so many ways, Father Young was just that, an exception.

If one was forced to put the blame squarely on anyone's shoulders, it would have to fall on Mother Young. Mothers carry a unique power over us, particularly those talented in the art of indoctrination. No mother had mastered this art more than Mother Young, and she had determined that her son would be a priest from the first morning she had nausea.

On May 27, 1530, Father Young came into the world. I say Father Young, but in his current position, he is officially, Father Father Young. It takes a special something to be so determined that your son will become a priest that you name him Father, and while it is unclear what that something is, Mother Young had it in basketfuls. Being the master of indoctrination that she was, Mother was also not blind to the fact that a parent's influence only goes so far. Yes, any parent knows that at some stage in their child's life, a parent's words somehow become like the speeches of royalty: you must attend but no one can make you listen. The real power then transfers to one's peers. Thus, it was the simple genius of her plot that her young son would hear, "Father, kick it my way," while he played kick-the-dirt-clod across the field, and "Father, can you pass me that jam?" at the dinner table. Indeed, one can only have every single person you encounter call you *Father* for so long before one day, in a flash of inspiration, you say, "Perhaps I shall devote myself to the church."

Even Father's Fathers were affected. Father MackleRoy, who began the instruction of little Father, could not help but see what Mother Young had forced on the world. Young Father was meant to be a priest, and the sooner he could *earn* this title, the less agitating it would be to address the young brute. Father MackleRoy once even contrived that if he should someday have a son, he would name him *Your Lordship MackleRoy* and send him to call upon Mother Young whenever he needed amusement. Of course, the plot was thwarted the very next moment by his sudden recollection of that awful word. Celibacy.

Exactly at which point Mother Young's ambition for her son became wholeheartedly his own we are left to conjecture, but we can, with conviction, say it did just that. Father became as devoted to the cloth as pigs are to mud. Fortunately, this transformation occurred at such an early age that celibacy, that shaker of men's souls, had never even stirred Father Young. He was celibate not only in act, but in thought. There was, of course, a room in his mind for such thoughts— there is in all our minds. He just never went in.

One would like to say that, in most cases, men found themselves rising to position in the clergy by inspiration and perspiration, but, in fact, it was mostly due to relation. Half-brothers to dukes needed something to occupy their time and so parishes were given out as birthday presents to those who missed the birthright for better positions. But once in a while, the man of merit gets a break, and such it was with Father Young. By this time, he had risen to his full stature being a quarter cubit taller than most men. His dark brown eyes and strong jaw did not match his mild manner, but while his handsome looks set him apart, it was more his dedication to the cloth that caught the eye of his superiors. And at the relatively young age of twenty-five, Father found himself officially titled Father Young, and found himself responsible for the parish and people in the small town of Bridgecrest.

The life of a priest suited Father and all too quickly he found himself settled. But, fate has a strong distaste for anything *settled*, and was already working towards the unsettling of things. And perhaps to ensure a hearty success, or perhaps because Father Young was incapable of suspecting anything under any circumstance, fate was concocting a means which Father Young would have never suspected: diseased pigs and love.

Amid the echoes of his own voice in a foreign tongue, Father Young heard the rusty door hinges announce the arrival of a latecomer. *Henry*, he thought, as he glanced down to mark his place in the recitation. Henry was the type of parishioner that believed if he ducked into church for five minutes, he could consider himself having attended and was thereby perfectly eligible for salvation. As this thought entered Father Young's mind, he realized it was far too early for Henry.

Instead, an unfamiliar family shuffled into his small chapel, and with them, a daughter. Father Young would never admit to it, but by 1557's standards, she was stunning. Rich brown eyes sat perfectly framed between her soft white cheeks and her bonnet. She swept aside a lock of rich, curled brown hair that playfully had escaped the bonnet's clutches revealing a shy smile and flushing cheeks. Even as she squeezed in front of displaced parishioners, she did so with grace. She stood a head taller than most of the women around her and was considerably more healthy in appearance—a picture of plumpness and beauty.

Upon seeing her, Father Young's heart leapt unexpectedly inside his chest, and he lost his place in Mass. Despite being the youngest priest in the diocese, this had never happened before. Father Young was a serious study, and, like many priests of his day, he took comfort in the fact that no one in his audience understood a word he was saying. Missing words here and there did not bother him, and he hoped the Good Lord would be as forgiving. This was different. He didn't know why he had stopped. But he certainly would not expect attraction.

When it came to attraction, Father Young had turned the key on that door before he knew the beast behind it. Asking Father Young if he was sad without attraction and its much more powerful companion, love, would be like asking him if he was disappointed that he could not use matches to light a fire. It was simply not a part of his life in any way. But unlike matches, love did exist in 1557, and even someone fairly oblivious was liable to be struck. Of course, someone who never expects to be in love can be taken somewhat off guard when it strikes. If you are struck on the head while walking and awaken on the ground an hour later, you may find it difficult to detect who or what had hit you. Most of us would look for our money purse, but finding it intact, we may resort to asking possible witnesses nearby or look for a rock or a meteorite in the general area. If none was to be found, the mystery may always remain just that.

Like the man lying knocked out, Father Young began to investigate. He must be ill, he thought, but if this was the case, he had recovered remarkably quickly and was now left looking for a meteorite.

Father Young's congregation may not have understood a word he was saying, but they did know pauses meant it was time to stand; so, the whole congregation was standing. Luckily, the embarrassment that ensued proved just the tonic he needed to rouse his faculties back to order, move past the mystery and begin again somewhere in the middle of Mass with no one being the wiser.

Father Young would have put this minor incident from his mind if it were not for its reoccurrence. While greeting those who had attended church, the new family approached him.

"Father Young, we are Mr. and Mrs. Porkshire. We recently moved from Lushton," the family's patriarch said as he approached the father.

"Did you say Porkshire?" Father Young asked.

"That's correct. My father was a pig farmer, his father was a pig farmer, and his father's father was a pig farmer. I think we have been farming pigs since we came through the Red Sea on dry ground."

Father Young debated noting that any Jewish ancestry this man had likely wasn't farming pigs but decided, "It's very good to meet you," was a safer choice.

"Truth is, Father, it's protecting my livelihood that made us move. Not too far out of Lushton, Mr. Hamstein's herd has been croaking right and left with some sort of plague. Figured it was safer to move than risk my babies. Father Young, do you like pork?"

"I . . . um . . ." Father Young hated to choose between a lie and the correct answer. "I guess I haven't had an opportunity to eat much pork."

"Well, we can change that." Mr. Porkshire launched into a long lecture on the general good health that comes from a diet rich in pork.

It clearly had made both him and his wife healthy, and then some. Father Young marveled that they appeared to possess enough health and everything else for two or three people. However, it was during Mr. Porkshire's sermon on the pork diet that Father Young's mind began to drift, and as the mind wandered, so did the eyes, and there she was again!

At the end of Mass many of the local children would come to gather their parents. There she was smiling and playing with the few of these children. A child had fallen, and she was holding and consoling her. Even as her focus was on the child in her arms, all the children beamed at her. Father Young too began to beam. Catching sight of this healthy—although much less than mom and papa—young lady, his heart leapt again.

One might assume that this second occurrence of heart aerobics, and both occurring when this maiden came into view, might tip Father Young off to the inconvenient truth that he was quickly falling for her. But he had almost thirty years of presuming, nah, *knowing* that he would never fall, and two five second occurrences, no matter how powerful, were not enough to change his mind.

Perhaps if he had more time to ponder on what had occurred, he would have solved the mystery, but before he could dwell on it any longer, Henry came running up to the church.

"Oh, Father, I'm right sorry for missin' service, but you know my cow got out of her pen again. And the Missus, she was havin' it at me! She says, 'Henry! If you fixed the gate proper when I axed you to!' . . ."

Despite Henry's considerable animation he exuberated while impersonating his wife's shrill voice, as his story wore on, the father's attention did not, and neither did his futile search for meteorites.

Chapter 2

A Priest in Love

Father Young's week continued much the same as every other week. Being a priest in the 16th century was not a recipe for a busy lifestyle. Most of his Sunday service was memorized or read, and the church required only light upkeep, with which he had help from his two deacons. The parish had its living quarters in the back, and beyond that lay a garden which Father Young kept more as a hobby than out of necessity. While he tried to keep it from going to his head, like most priests, he was the richest man in town. What the clergy lacked in love, it made up for in pay.

Besides a few sessions of confession and the selling of indulgences, he was pretty free to do as he chose. He kept several hobbies, in addition to gardening. He also enjoyed reading and had built up quite a library, but when reading or gardening did not suit his fancy, he would spend some time visiting members of his congregation.

This particular week, he had just finished a book, and it was too cold to garden, so he decided to make some visits. *Perhaps I should visit the new family, the Porkshires?* he thought. It is important to remember that the poor man did not know his true feelings. If he had known them, he would have stayed far away from the Porkshires. Not only was he a priest, but even a man of steel can be reduced to jelly when around the woman he admires. Those in love must constantly struggle between the desire to see their love and their dislike of existing in a gelatinous state. Father Young had the blessing of not knowing he was falling for the daughter and so he naively said to himself, *Of course, I'll visit the Porkshires. They are new and in need of fellowship.*

As Mr. Porkshire had expressed to Father Young, pig farming was in his blood, and as such, Mr. Porkshire was no amateur at picking a location for his swine. Out on the edge of town was a large plot of land left vacant for years. The green hills of Bridgecrest were of the perfect rolling grass covered variety except for one blemish, its muddy armpit. A low spot among the hills of Bridgecrest, the ugly duckling of Bridgecrest landscapes, was perpetually covered in mud. Excessive muddiness, while not appreciated by farmers, is well appreciated by pigs, and Mr. Porkshire was a 'pigs first' kind of farmer.

As the road crested over the last hill, Father Young noted how quickly Mr. Porkshire had altered the landscape that now graced his eyes. The mud was as abundant as ever, a thick slog where the water and dirt could find no way to divorce each other and just became thicker and deeper with each passing season. But now its perimeter was marked by evenly spaced log posts with thin timber rails stretched between, which seemed a futile attempt to entrap this now precious mud that never leaves.

At the center of it all, now stood an island of rocks and boulders mounded up to support the small timber cottage that stood as a bold affront of civility to the encompassing slog that wanted to swallow it.

It was a typical one-bedroom shack affair, but one that would likely still be standing after a few puffs from a local wolf. The entire scene was a testament to the hardworking nature of the family. It was no castle but the fact that it all came forth from the mud in less than a week impressed Father Young. But as he drew closer, a new impression forced itself upon him, starting at his nose. The mud was clearly made of more than dirt and water, and the acidic stench seared his nostrils.

As he approached, animal forms became clear in the surrounding yard. Father Young saw at least fifty pigs, but soon reduced his estimate to forty-nine when number fifty lifted itself from all fours and stood on its hind legs. It was Mr. Porkshire, who clearly shared his pigs' affinity for mud.

"Good Morning, Father Young!" he said without a hint of embarrassment for having been bathing in the mud. He thrust his hand forward toward Father Young in order to clasp his guest's as any kind host would. The thick cake mixed with chunks of rotting food dripped off the hand. Father Young was not really a fan of hand shaking even when the hand wasn't covered with the dregs of a pig's bath, but he could not grasp a way out, so he shook. However, you could not say he actually shook Mr. Porkshire's hand as he was fairly confident their hands made no contact through the mud, excrement, and food barrier. Father Young's hand slid back and forth in the slime as they shook. Upon separating, Father Young gave his wrist a few quick flicks, trying unsuccessfully to clear the mud.

"That there is good honest earth and water, in their greatest form, mud. Can't you just feel the life in it?" Mr. Porkshire said after noting Father Young's vain attempts at clearing his hand.

Father Young was not sure what he was feeling but sincerely hoped there was not much living going on in it.

Father Young was finding it difficult to respond to Mr. Porkshire. While Father Young stood in shock, Mr. Porkshire took the opportunity to explain what he was doing. "Father Young, if you was wondering why I was on all fours, well I was testing the depth of mud. See, pigs like to sink approximately one hand depth into the mud when on their side."

Mr. Porkshire was a man that clearly outpaced society. If he had only been born later, he would have been a well published professor on the subject of swine farming. He was avid at determining, in every way, the best methods for raising his swine. Had Father Young made a closer examination, he would have noticed that the house was surrounded with four separate pens, each with a similar number of pigs. Mr. Porkshire was currently in the midst of experimenting with different feeds and how they affected the growth and flavor of the pig. Father Young's ignorance of this important scientific undertaking was remedied when Mr. Porkshire concluded his lecture on mud depth and began educating his visitor on the relative merits of various feed types.

It was during this topic that Father Young's mind began to wander again. The act of allowing his mind to wander during a lecture on

swine reminded him that last time this occurred he was looking at—
what was it?—*the daughter.* The thought caused his heart a minor skip,
nothing like the leap that looking at the real thing did, but something
moved within him, nonetheless. As usual, he was in denial. Father
Young only realized that he was desirous to see her and interrupted
Mr. Porkshire mid-lecture, "Are your wife and daughter at home?"

"I do slaughter at home . . . oh, what?" Mr. Porkshire paused and
looked back at the house as if he hadn't seen it before. "Oh! The wife
is here, but my daughter, Fannie, she's out and about." The enthusiasm
in his voice was gone. He knew his talk of pigs was over.

Fannie had spent most of her time out and about since they came to
Bridgecrest. After having spent her morning helping her father care-
fully weigh out four sets of different feeds, she kissed him on the
cheek and bolted toward the nearby hills. Her athletic legs carried
her quickly down a dirt path which led to a large meadow. She had
found this clearing in the hills the day they had moved to Bridgecrest.
Nature was her sanctuary, and since moving, she needed sanctuary.
Fannie had spent her whole life living in a palace of optimism, but
she could feel the walls cracking. She had been content to allow her
parents to make most of her decisions, but she could sense that the
arrangement couldn't last forever. When they had told her they were
moving from Lushton to Bridgecrest to protect the pigs, she did what
she always did, smiled and graciously obeyed. Inside however, things
were different. Secretly she wrestled with a new emotion best described
as resentment. She couldn't help her mind from asking questions like,
*What about my life here? Were you going to ask me? Do my thoughts and
desires matter?* And she realized that for the first time in her life she
wanted a vote, and more importantly something inside her told her
she was of age to deserve one.

Pigs were going to move her away from the town she had known
her whole life. Away from friends, her favorite aunt, and the young
men in the town she was becoming acquainted with . . . for pigs?
Shouldn't her parents care as much about her thoughts as they did for
the pigs? On the road to this new town, she repressed these thoughts

and never mentioned a word of it to her parents. After all, they were in charge, and it was her job to be the obedient daughter.

She now went to the edge of the meadow where the trees cast long shadows and sat in their shade looking closely at a stem of the little white flowers with red bulbs behind them. Enchanter's nightshade, her favorite flower, they always grew under the shade of large trees, not out in the open. *That was me*, she thought, *Always in the shade of my parents*. She now added vocally, "Perhaps it's time I saw the sun," as she rose and ran towards the sunshine of the open meadow.

As she ran, she continued to think about how her parents hadn't even asked her about moving for the sake of the pigs. Clearly, she saw who was more important. A realization was growing in her, something that had been growing for many years despite her trying to suppress it. And most importantly, it solidified one thing that she could sense was growing for a long time. As the air danced through her hair, she allowed herself to admit it for the first time. First in her thoughts, then under her breath, and soon with a lightened heart she was yelling out loud, "I am a Porkshire, and I hate pigs!"

Back at the homestead, Mr. Porkshire was disappointed to be moving from the comfort of his mud bath, but even pig farmers sometimes know what customary hospitality requires. "I suppose you'd like to come inside?" he said, as he gestured to Father Young.

Father Young nodded and headed to the small shack. As he drew near, he was able to get a closer look at the little shack. It wasn't much different from any shack at the time but it was the small differences that mattered. The edges created a line as straight as a pig's tail was curly. The sun glinted off the thick thatched roof. It overhung the shack by almost a cubit. How they could get it to stay in place for that long was a mystery to Father, and he was tempted to reach up and feel it as they drew near. Getting that kind of overhang would be useful. Father Young regularly saw shacks around town appear to melt in the frequent rains as mud placed between logs gave way to God's tears. The most impressive piece of the Porkshire's handiwork was what Mr.

Porkshire reached for now—the front door. As far as doors go it was very bland, but the fact that it existed at all was a surprise.

Mr. Porkshire had hardly laid a hand on the latch when a voice called out, "Don't you thinks of coming in this house with your boots on!" It was Mrs. Porkshire, the domicile's only defense against the ever-invading wetland.

"The Missus don't care for the good earth," whispered Mr. Porkshire.

Father Young assumed it wasn't the good earth that Mrs. Porkshire didn't care for as much as the way it clung to the straw on her floor. Mr. Porkshire removed his boots, but even if all his clothing had been removed, plenty of the good earth would have still been with him.

The moment they entered, Father Young could tell Mrs. Porkshire did not share Mr. Porkshire's affinity for mud. The cottage was as clean as any shack could make itself.

"Oh, Father Young! How good of you to come! I told ya he was a good one," she said, smacking Mr. Porkshire across the chest. "Comin' to see us as soon as we settled in. I'm honored!"

"Sit down, sit down." She motioned to a little table with four stools around it. The room barely had space enough for the table, and Father Young doubted it could also accommodate Mr. and Mrs. Porkshire on each end of it. What he did not account for was the ability of Mr. and Mrs. Porkshire's robust figures to morph into whatever shape sturdy walls and furniture demanded. As Mr. Porkshire squeezed between the table and his stool, the table scraped mud from his belly, piling it onto the place in front of him. Once settled, he swept the pile onto the floor. Mrs. Porkshire turned her head and cringed.

Collecting herself, she asked, "Father, would you care for a steak from the hindquarter, or a few slices of bacon?"

Father Young thanked her but passed and prepared to be eloquent. When visiting new members of his flock, Father Young delivered a prepared speech about how he would do his best to be a good shepherd, borrowing heavily from the Gospel of John. It was intended to make newcomers feel welcome, but as he spoke, Mr. Porkshire's face and indeed his whole body began to squirm.

It was no fault of Father Young's, but Mr. Porkshire, while fine with religion, had a difficult time with much of the Bible. From the little he knew of it, he felt pork was given a raw deal.

In the Old Testament, God forbade its consumption, and then once the New Testament comes around, he was always praising sheep and shepherds. Why didn't pig farmers behold the new star or hear angels? When it came to the story of Christ casting out spirits and allowing them to enter a herd of swine, his sympathies sided with the farmer who watched his pigs fling themselves into the sea. And casting pearls before swine might have been a good source of minerals if they weren't so hard on their molars.

Father Young had no idea of the pain he was causing as he waxed on about shepherds and sheep, and he would have continued, but then Fannie came home. Not knowing of Father Young's presence, she entered exactly how she usually did, dancing and humming to herself. She opened the door, and before anyone could warn her, she spun around saying, "Mama and Papa, the meadow was so beautiful today!"

Fannie's dress rose up almost to her knees as she spun, slightly exposing the hem of her underdress. Father Young tried hard not to notice and quickly stood as he turned his head. The action had potential to succeed if it hadn't been for the tight quarters. The stool tried unsuccessfully to get out of the way of the rising priest. The noise of the stool as it hit the wall and ground and splintered into several pieces got Fannies attention.

She stopped her spin "I'm so sorry, Father Young. I didn't know you were here," she said as her cheeks grew flushed.

"Father was just telling us about sheep herding," said Mrs. Porkshire. "Why don't you join us dear?"

Still blushing, eyes downcast, Fannie pulled up the last stool and sat.

The point of his speech may have eluded Mrs. Porkshire, but at that moment she had a better grasp on the subject than did Father Young. He remained standing, as the only stool left no longer was up to the task of holding him or anyone else. Father Young had visited the Porkshire's on the rather innocent premise of welcoming them to the Parish, but now as his legs turned to jelly and his heart raced, he was beginning to question his decision. But more pressingly, as three smiling faces looked up at him, he knew he needed to say something.

"Well, you know, the Lord has said . . ." The phrase came out slowly and awkwardly, and while it seemed a safe direction to head, at the moment, he couldn't think of a single thing the Lord *had* said. After considerable pause, he recited the only scripture that came to his mind, "For this cause shall a man leave his father and his mother and cleave unto his wife and none else." He instantly realized that it wasn't appropriate, but he left it at that.

Luckily, Mrs. Porkshire liked this as much as anything about sheep, and Mr. Porkshire liked it considerably more.

They may have sat in silence for a long time had Mr. Porkshire not spoken up. "Father Young, do you think they could have gotten sheep and swine mixed up when they translated the Bible?"

The question allowed Father Young to momentarily come to himself long enough to say that he found it unlikely, thank the Porkshires for their kindness, and ask to be excused.

"Thank you so much for coming, Father," Mr. Porkshire said as he, his wife, and Fannie arose.

It was as Fannie arose that Father Young realized he would have to walk right by her in order to reach the door.

He smiled, turned to the door, and repeated in his head as he made small steps between deep breaths, *Don't turn your head, focus on the door. On the door, you can do it.*

About a mile down the road, Father Young felt his heart and breath slow down and his legs begin to solidify. Thoughts ran too fast for his brain to catch hold of them. The twirl, the face, the hair, the leaping and skipping of his heart, his loss of speech and mental capacity, the numbness in his lower limbs all added up to something. As he slowly put the pieces together, one by one, he could deny it no longer: he was a priest, and he was in love.

Chapter 3

A Soused Bishop

ather Young was not the first priest torn between love of the cloth and love of a woman. For hundreds of years, men chased the priesthood; some for God, some for gold, and some who didn't know what else to do. For whatever reason, a portion find themselves still afflicted with this human condition. Many are apt to wonder why Paul ever said to the Corinthians, "I say therefore to the unmarried . . . it is good for them." Some of those experiencing what was, "good for them" conjectured that Paul must have possessed an uncommon abundance of optimism. But it was what it was, and for the privilege of the Priesthood, celibacy was a worthwhile price to pay—or at least that is what they said to console themselves on lonely nights—which was every night.

Fifteen years earlier, in a nearby town, another member of the cloth suffered with a similar struggle. Father Goldheart had just become Bishop Goldheart at the young age of thirty. The honor of going from a priest that oversaw a parish to a bishop who had ecclesiastical authority over a diocese made up of many parishes was naturally an honor, but not one without merit. This early advancement presented itself because no one worked harder or related better to his flock than Father Goldheart. Once a priest, his sincere love for his flock, both attendees and absentees, was evident. It was just as likely to find Father Goldheart at the local tavern as at the chapel. His purpose and his consumption contrasted with the general tavern goer. He'd float from table to table with, "How's the Missus? I saw your fence broke, can I help? Missed you on Sunday, everything okay?" And "Who's this? I thought you were married." He knew many who wandered into the tavern were doing the same in their spiritual walk, wandering. A wise shepherd who has lost his sheep would naturally begin his search near the river, as a straying lamb would be drawn to it. This tavern was just such a river for thirsty sheep, and unfortunately, he knew many would slip off the banks and drown if he didn't come to coax them home. His efforts were not in vain, and attendance at Mass swelled, and of greater note to his superiors, so did the offerings on the collection plate.

Bishop Hoodlenip had overseen the lone Cathedral in Lushton ever since his brother, Duke Hoodlenip, had demanded such. Since Bishop Hoodlenip had assumed the position, attendance and offerings had gone in the opposite direction to what they had for Father Goldheart. As their superiors began to notice Father Goldheart's success, they equally, if not more so, noted Bishop Hoodlenip's failure. After all, the Cathedral was the largest congregation in the diocese and many observed the income drop not only on paper, but in their purse. The lightened purses of the leadership sealed Hoodlenip's fate. He had to go, the further the better. Therefore, as soon as a promotion to Cardinal opened up, his name was given with the highest recommendations.

Father Goldheart was an obvious choice to replace Bishop Hoodlenip, hence *Bishop* Goldheart was born. Upon arriving at Lushton, he wasted no time. Before he had even unpacked his belongings, he was determined to get out among his flock. Most villages had a large inn and tavern at the center of town, and Lushton was no exception. The bishop found the inn exactly where he expected, and in he went.

A bewildered Bishop Goldheart found himself staring into a near-empty room. There was only one solitary man: a large, gruff-looking barkeep who sat behind the counter scrubbing mugs. A tavern with no people! The very thought made him quiver. A town where taverns sat empty may be some clergyman's dream, but for him, it was simply a waste of talent. But before he resigned his new post, he had to investigate.

"Good afternoon!"

A glance and a grumble replaced a civil reply.

"How are you?"

"Who's askin'?"

"I apologize. I haven't introduced myself. I'm Father . . . I mean Bishop Goldheart, and I will be at the Cathedral down the road taking the place of—"

"Enough!" the barkeep roared and raised an enormous hand. Given the barkeeper's lack of interest in any backstory there was little else for the bishop to say. He had many more questions but this man must have learned customer service from an undertaker. Nevertheless, after a healthy pause, curiosity overruled hesitancy.

"So, where is everybody?"

The man looked up glaring and sighed. "Do you want to buy a drink or not?"

When someone said, "Brevity is the soul of wit," he had clearly not met the Lushton barkeeper. Now grateful he had failed to close the door, Bishop saw some folks passing by and decided now was the time to withdraw from his current company. "No, thank you, not today," he said as he made his exit.

Luckily for the bishop, the two gentlemen in whose company he now found himself were much more approachable. They were reluctant to speak casually with the clergy, particularly a bishop, mostly because their only previous encounters with one were from the confines of a confession box. Any experience that takes our memory back to confession has a tendency to make us uneasy, but the bishop's easygoing way with them was disarming.

"So, I just came from the inn and it seemed rather sparse, the attendance, that is."

"The inn? Oh, no one goes to the inn, unless they have to. In Lushton, everyone goes to Denine's Tavern."

"Where is that?"

"We were just on our way there to get a . . . to meet a friend." They had grown more comfortable with the bishop, but he was still a bishop.

They led him to the edge of town and into a wooded area. He was surprised any establishment existed this far out of town. He grew even more surprised as he peered through the woods and still could see no tavern. The trio weaved down a long path through the woods until finally, a quaint, cottage-like building came into view. A sign that simply read, "Denine's," hung over the door. Though cottage-like in its dark wood framing and thatched roof it was actually quite large, and as they entered, Bishop Goldheart understood why. The place had no shortage of customers. There were people in every nook and cranny eating, drinking, talking, singing and dancing. Bishop Goldheart suddenly felt very differently about Lushton. This town was chock-full of his sort of people: great people who just needed to see the joys of the gospel.

The tavern had a long bar and was filled with sturdy, nicely carved tables and chairs. Wood floors, a luxury rarely found in taverns of the day, not only existed but actually looked clean. *Who was this Mr. Denine?* he thought as he found a seat amid the patrons at the largest table. "Hello, Brother," he said, turning to a young fellow at his right. The entire table and several tables nearby instantly fell silent. No one, save the two gentlemen who had accompanied him, knew who he was, but he was obviously clergy. And a clergy member pushing his way into a tavern was definitely not a welcome sight. Drinking was not condemned in the church, after all, wine was given each week as part of communion. But drinking for fun or in excess, while not forbidden, was heavily discouraged. Most priests frankly condemned it. Even priests who enjoyed the drink themselves avoided taverns, preferring to participate in a personal communion in the privacy of their own homes.

"Well," Bishop Goldheart continued, "What are you drinking?"

The man stammered somewhat and hid his mug. "Tea."

"Tea! Let me get you a real drink!" He then turned to the barmaid, "Ma'am . . ." As his eyes connected with hers, he lost his caravan of thought. He was lost in her deep brown eyes. Freckles graced her fair skin and her long auburn hair filled him with fire. He turned his head away, took a deep breath and turning back said, "Get my friend here one of your best ales."

Nothing could have broken the ice more effectively, and in an instant, the eating, drinking, singing and dancing picked up where they had stopped. The only difference was that all the conversations were now about him. *Who was this priest? What kind of clergyman would act like this?* It wasn't long before everyone knew that no one knew who the bishop was. Finally, someone asked the one man who did know, "So, Father, are you just passing through?"

"No, I've just been ordained to replace Bishop Hoodlenip here in Lushton." Not a soul knew who Hoodlenip was, not even those who had lived in the town for decades, but they understood that this intriguing stranger was not only clergy, but a bishop, and more importantly, their bishop.

Bishop Goldheart quickly became acquainted with all the men at his table. None of them were the type that would admit wanting to know a bishop but associating with someone of his rank lent a sense of pride as intoxicating as their ale. Particularly, as most of them would be going home to a wife—a wife who may not be too keen on where they had been. Now they looked forward to reporting, "I was spending time getting to know our new bishop."

Throughout the night, he could not help but observe the beautiful barmaid who had first caught his eye. She demonstrated far more experience and responsibility than your average maid. She seemed to be managing the other staff and handling most customer questions. He began to wonder if this could be Mrs. Denine, the wife of the owner. But her age made that unlikely, that is, if her husband was anywhere near her age, he would be awfully young to own such a place. Then again, given how busy this place was, he was likely a man of means and could afford the luxury of a young bride.

"Excuse me, ma'am. Where might I find Mr. Denine?"

"There is no Mr. Denine," she said, not turning to look at him as she wiped a mug dry with the towel she always kept with her.

"Oh, is Denine not the owner's name?"

She thumped her mug down and flipped the towel onto her shoulder, her brown eyes turned brazen and locked onto Bishop. "No, it is."

"Then who is the owner of this fine establishment?"

"I am *Miss* Denine," she said as she went back to drying mugs.

Bishop Goldheart had guessed her name correctly but had not guessed the proper title. And that difference between Mrs. and Miss was a wide gulf indeed. Silence did little to mask his shock. He could not comprehend it. Someone so beautiful, so young, so single, and so female, how could she own so much? Indeed, you might as well have told him that Henry VIII had become celibate. But here he was, and there she stood. As soon as he was able to suspend disbelief, he smiled and said, "Congratulations, my dear! Very impressive! You have done a marvelous job with this place."

Miss Denine was accustomed to dealing with those who could not believe she was the owner, but they had never turned to a positive reaction so quickly. Most could barely hide their initial disapproval, and some were so upset they had to be thrown out. Usually they would be so mad that they would actually take their business to the local inn at least once or twice before the innkeeper's notorious customer service sent them back to Miss Denine's hospitality. It was actually this inability for men to grasp the concept of female ownership that had led to the tavern's woodsy location. No woman was allowed to officially own or even lease land, so she had to build outside the city on unregulated property.

The bishop's positive response was almost as shocking to her as her ownership was to him. "Thank you," was her only vocal response. But as she turned to respond to one of the almost constant calls for her help across the tavern, she also gave a smile. Miss Denine was not a somber person, and she was often seen with a smile, but this smile was something different. And she felt her face blush realizing how she had just smiled at a bishop. She wondered if that was a sin, and the very thought of having to see him in confession warmed her again.

The next morning the bishop's aching head let him know he had taken his duties a little too far last night. Yet despite the pain, he had great hope for Lushton. That became clearer as he walked toward the pulpit a few hours later to begin Mass, as seated on the front row was the smiling face of the barmaid. Her pew and the two behind her were filled with the roughest crew Bishop Goldheart had ever seen in any sacred edifice.

The bishop's favorite verse of scripture had always been, "What man of you, having an hundred sheep, if he lose one of them, doth not leave the ninety and nine in the wilderness, and go after that which is lost, until he find it? And when he hath found it, he layeth it on his shoulders, rejoicing."

As Bishop Goldheart looked at the hair of flames in the front pew, he wondered if he had found the one.

Miss Denine and Bishop quickly became a great team. She became a regular at his Cathedral and he became even more regular at her tavern. Soon, those who oversaw the Diocese were very pleased that attendance was once again on the rise, and rising with it, of course, were the offerings. However, even before Newton had said it, what goes up doesn't stay that way.

In this case, the down came the day the bishop had the same realization that Father Young would have fifteen years later: he was in love. Miss Denine wasn't just the one to help him gather his lost sheep, but she was the one in so many other ways. And more importantly, the one in the only way that was beginning to matter in the bishop's life. With this realization, Bishop Goldheart found himself less focused on all he had and more focused on what he could never have: Miss Denine. Over time, he was increasingly depressed as he walked to the tavern each day. He did not like this new self. But he found that if he picked up a few more drinks, his old jovial nature would return. Before long, he required more and more drinks, which began earlier and earlier in the day.

Pretty soon, he had forgotten what Paul had said to Timothy about bishops in chapter seven, that they should not be given to wine. Someone had once pointed this out to him, and after sobering up, he read the chapter and noticed that Paul also said bishops should be, "The husband of one wife." He determined Paul was right, and if he had his one wife, then he wouldn't be given to wine.

Miss Denine's feelings for the bishop began with that smile and only grew from there. She knew it didn't do any good, so neither he nor she ever spoke of it. But while she could not speak of her love, she could always come to his aid. If you were to enter the tavern on any day but Sunday, you were likely to find the bishop laughing and jesting beyond sober limits. On occasion, a traveler, judgmental bunch that they are, would come through and say to Miss Denine, "That's the bishop? I can't believe it's tolerated for a man of the cloth to appear in such a state!"

She'd snap back, "Why, it's his duty to be that way! You know there be two types of drunks: them that's somber and remorseful, and them that let the liquor of life pick them up and get jovial. Why, the bishop's not the same man without a drink or two. And what of it? If you could be so good a bishop as him and all it took was a little liquid nourishment, then it'd be your duty as a man of the cloth to drink it! He is twice the man you are, drunk or sober, now get out!"

Bishop Goldheart was not as merciful to himself, and in his rare sober moments, he knew he was not the man he should be. But he found it difficult to care. Secretly, he hoped they would defrock him, and he'd be free to marry Miss Denine. But he knew it was the 1550's, and being a drunk may keep you from becoming a bishop but was not nearly enough to change the fact that you were one.

Bishop Goldheart felt hopeless. The core of hope is the idea that you can do something to improve the situation. No action he could conceive would improve it. When others were hopeless, he used to say, "God will make it right in the end," but even in that sentiment he now wavered. The only "make it right" he could figure was to marry Miss Denine, but he knew the clergy were, "neither married nor given in marriage."

So, there he sat for fifteen years, fluctuating between sober and sad, and drunk and happy.

It was in the sober and sad state that Father Young hoped to find him on the cold morning in 1557 when he came to see the bishop. Father

Young, like everyone else in town, was aware of the bishop's situation, or at least the outward expression of it.

Father Young set out the day before and spent the night at the local inn because Lushton was about a day's journey from Bridgecrest. Knowing the bishop's routine allowed Father Young to know exactly where to find him. He had come for advice. Once he had realized he was in love, he was at a loss as to the right thing to do. Should he avoid Fannie completely, or try to see her and simply overcome his feelings? In his weaker moments, he debated confessing to her in order to warn her that his avoidance was due to love, not hatred. Deep down he knew that telling her would be wrong. That didn't stop him from thinking about it.

After debating between several options, he decided that the right course of action, no matter how awkward it would be, was to discuss the situation with his spiritual leader. He knew that the bishop spent much of his life walking resolutely to the tavern and then staggering back home, but he was still his spiritual guide whom God had called, so he proceeded with faith in his drunken leader. In this, Father Young was unique. Not many men will make a day's journey to seek a drunk's advice because it's the right thing to do.

Father Young chose to spend the night at the inn to allow sleep to sober the bishop. Not that the Lord couldn't inspire a drunk, the Lord could do anything, but his faith was too weak for such a miracle. As he saw the bishop stagger back to the cathedral from the inn's upper window, he knew his decision to wait until morning was a good one.

As he stepped into Denine's tavern the next morning, he wondered if he had slept too long. Would the bishop have already enjoyed the view of an empty glass or two?

What he didn't know was that the bishop, while known as a drunk, enjoyed the clarity of mind that sobriety brought for several hours every morning.

He would sit in the tavern in the early hours and soberly wallow in his predicament. Seeing Miss Denine, saying, "good morning," to her, and even from time to time, if business was slow, actually having a conversation with her, became his daily routine. He both loved and hated these hours. Hating the pathetic lump of remorse that he had become was balanced with the satisfaction one gets from wallowing.

The bishop still had a good hour of wallowing left when Father Young approached. "Bishop Goldheart!"

"Oh, Father Young, what brings you to our village?" Despite wallowing at present, he was always kind and even sounded happy to see the priest.

"I was wondering if we could talk."

"Of course, we can talk—all day if you'd like! Shall I buy you a drink?" He knew his wallowing was over so decided he might as well move on to phase two.

"I think I'd prefer it if we met back at the cathedral," Father Young said timidly.

"Oh, yes . . . of course." The bishop did not like this turn of events. Up to this point he assumed Father Young may have come to try the local cuisine, but to meet at the cathedral meant two things: one, he had come to confess, and a priest was rarely moved by inward conviction to confess. Priests believed themselves to be righteous; after all, they are priests, and the higher the position, the further from humility they ascended. Usually, if a priest was confessing, it was only after the town was aware of his indiscretion and a scandal had ensued. When Father Mistrol had been caught stealing chickens from the locals, Bishop Goldheart had to send him to Sheldon, the furthest parish on the edge of his diocese where chickens had been banished by an allergy-afflicted nobility. This was not only a grand nuisance, but he then had to relocate the priest in Sheldon who was a good man and loved his parish. He was in no state to be rearranging parishes, but while this fear lingered in the back of his mind, it was still overshadowed by the second thing this meant. His day was going to be largely void of both Miss Denine and all the consoling products she served.

So, Bishop Goldheart and Father Young began toward the church. A little small talk was shared, but mostly they walked in silence. Both had things to occupy their minds. For Bishop Goldheart, they say absence makes the heart grow fonder, and absence from drink had already started to work its magic.

For Father Young, one might think he would have already constructed exactly what he was going to say after an entire day's walk, but they'd be wrong. His mind was still rehearsing different options. So, both his and the bishop's minds were occupied, and a busy mind makes silence quite bearable. Not to mention that priests typically struggle with small talk anyway. Humans naturally draw from several things when forced to converse with those they do not know well. The go-to option is the weather, but rarely does it lead to much more than additional awkward pauses. The second option that might follow is, "How are your wife and children?" So, you can see how small talk was difficult among priests.

Upon entry, the bishop headed straight to the confession box. He was halfway in when Father Young stopped him, "Bishop, I don't think I need confession today." Bishop Goldheart was both pleased and confused. This meant no rearranging of the parishes, but if confession was not required, why was he not having this conversation in the tavern over a drink or two?

"Well, shall we sit down?" They sat in the pew closest to them.

"Bishop, I'm not sure how to ask this," started Father Young. There was a long pause. Bishop Goldheart had learned not to fear long pauses in such situations. They were the only way to allow the reluctant speaker to get it out.

"Well . . . see . . . there is a good family that just moved into my parish, and they have a daughter."

Sounds simple enough, lots of families do, thought the bishop, continuing his silence.

"And I find myself . . . moved by her."

Bishop Goldheart was unsure if it was due to his age or his profession, but he didn't know what "moved by her" was supposed to mean. "You mean she bothers you. You want to move?" Thoughts of parish shake-ups again jostled his nerves.

"No, not that . . . I believe I am attracted to her," Father Young said.

Now the bishop was in trouble. Not only did he have no idea what to tell him, but he was probably the worst man to ask for any advice on the subject.

"Well, didn't you say she just moved in?"

"Yes."

The bishop sympathized with love but did not understand love at first sight. He saw love taking time and depth, could he even really call it love? In some ways he thought the father was somewhat naïve. "This may pass. I find nothing wrong with you noticing a pretty face."

Father Young shifted in his seat. "The problem is, I love her."

When we believe we are coming off too weak, we tend to overcorrect. Father Young had now come off too strong. He should have said he thought he loved her, and the bishop would have sympathized as a fellow conflicted brother, but this had the opposite effect.

The bishop gave him a chiding look that said, "How could you say you love her? What do you know of love? For fifteen years I have suffered true love, and you come to me having seen a pretty face, felt a mild tremor, and fancy yourself in love!" Bishop Goldheart was known for his long-winded looks, but some of this rebuke was lost in translation by Father Young who detected only severe displeasure. But before repeating himself out loud, Bishop Goldheart found the strength to step back and realize that, naïve as Father Young may be, here was a good man simply asking for advice.

Taking a deep breath, he made further inquiry, "How well do you know her?"

"I'll admit this all sounds a bit silly. I guess I don't know her that well. I just feel strange when I see her, and I don't know whether to avoid her or try to act like nothing is happening."

Now the bishop saw the full picture and contemplated his advice. One should not misjudge the bishop. After all, this is the longest stretch of sobriety he'd had in quite some time, and his mental acuity may have suffered more than those more accustomed to a clear head. "See her as much as possible," he began. "Get to know her as best you can. This may not be a problem at all. You might find you hate her! How can we deal with this unless we know you're really in love?"

Whether the bishop actually assumed this would lead the priest to indifference about the girl, or whether he, being miserable, desired a mutually miserable companion, we cannot be sure. But that was the advice, and it was warmly received by its surprised recipient.

Father Young beamed with a smile and relief but then his face turned sour just as quickly, "But what if I find I do love her?"

This part was uncomfortable. The most apparent answer of, "move to Lushton and wallow in sorrow with me," wouldn't do, so the bishop simply said, "Let's find out if you really love the girl before we get too worried."

Both men rose and walked together much more happily as they headed back through town. The bishop was so pleased to see the positive effect of his advice that he decided to spend the rest of the day sober, a resolution that sank in so deep, it lasted nearly an hour after the two men parted.

Father Young had not expected this advice and it gave him hope, perhaps short lived, but hope, nonetheless. He now had an action to perform that might solve his issue. Part of him hoped that he would realize that he did not like her. Perhaps she was a stumbling dolt, a very beautiful one but a dolt nonetheless. He didn't know. Perhaps she loved pigs as much as her dear old papa. But part of this hope, though not consciously admitted, derived from the seemingly impossible unification of his clerical duty and his innermost desires to spend time with Fannie. He now had a day's journey to plan how to accomplish his next task—getting to know Miss Fannie Porkshire.

Chapter 4

A Peasant Reporter

To understand the next part of our tale, I must pause and give a short history lesson. The cold hard facts of who was king and queen and what they did in England from 1530-1557, where we find ourselves, are well documented. But facts are not the whole of history.

Henry and Edward both lived in Bridgecrest and were the best of friends. Both were simpleminded men who enjoyed spending most of their day talking. They were better suited for the halls of Parliament than as farmers where they found themselves. Further evidence to their natural affinity for politics was the fact that both were farmers but *talked* more of farming than they actually *did* farming. This wouldn't have been so bad if they had ever talked of farming, but there were far more important things to consume their conversations. They preferred to be big picture types and left the day-to-day farming, and all other work, to their wives. After all, big picture people can't be bothered with actual work.

While much of Bridgecrest was concerned with whether their potatoes had sufficient water, Henry and Edward speculated about more important things such as whether or not the local duke, Duke Diddlehop, was going to summer in London or if Queen Mary would have a baby. The only source of such information was the occasional traveler. The problem with the occasional traveler was that they were only accurate about 50% of the time, which in the case of a two-option scenario, such as whether the queen was pregnant, offered the same reliability as a coin flip. But no one would be so foolish as to relay news discovered directly by coin flipping, so passing travelers it was. Henry and Edward were anxious to relay such discoveries and dealt with the 50% problem by assuming whatever they heard was true and that no one was likely to discover otherwise, except, of course, by coin flipping.

This had made the past few years of their lives rather exciting. There were two general perspectives on rulers in England. Many in the King's court and those living near London disliked King Henry VIII. He was an embarrassment, and his actions had deteriorated relations with Spain, the church, and just about everyone else. This is all well-known and understood, but then there was the perspective of those who shared Henry and Edward's view. In their mind, no king could compare with King Henry. While he reigned, the world was full of buzz and excitement. It all started one day when Edward came running up to Henry's shack. And anything that could motivate Edward to be running, Henry knew must be good.

"What ya be huffin in for?" Henry asked.

"You be happy when you 'ear about this!"

"What?"

"It's just like you says."

"Well, I says a lot in me days, so what about?"

"Promise me an ale and I will relay."

Becoming a paid informant was a coveted job back then. "Ah, ale? You comes down here all huff, clearly wantin' to tell me, you dangle a bit of goods, and then ask for an ale? I knows you want to tell me. Why should I pay to give yous what you want when I'm 'ere ready to listen. Plus, whatever yous got to tell me, I's the one that gave it to ya 'cause you said I already says it!" Henry said as he tilted his head towards Edward daring him to countermand him.

"Fine." Henry always was the better debater. "Ol' King 'Enry's done with the Spanish dame."

This brightened Henry's mood. "Just like I says, How'd you like being married to a dame who can't even talks to ya?"

As the words left his mouth, he realized that there was an upside to this, so he added, "Not only that, she's nothin' for him, she was 'is brother's bride. You want your brother's old widow?"

"The Bible does say . . ." started Edward.

"Da bible!" Henry shot back, "What's the Bible gots to do with it? Why bring religion in this? He don't want her, and that's that. Why should he be forced? If I was king, no one would be forcing me!"

"That may be, but religion got an awful lots to do with it, 'cause the Pope says, 'What God hath stuck together, no Pope can pull apart.'" The Bible had only been translated into English twenty-five years previously, but Edward was already providing a modernized edition.

Henry wouldn't even let scripture slow him down. "Listen, if you's was to look up King in a book, you'd see they says, 'Boss; Top of the World.' And then in big letters it would say, 'No bloke tells him what to do! Not even the Pope!'"

Edward, who had always been more religiously inclined than Henry, opened his mouth in shock. "I wouldn't be going around callin the Holy Father bloke. And not only that, you and King Henry ever hear of excommunion?"

"What?"

"Excommunion. It means you're cut off—no longer a good Christian, not even Catholic. That means everybody else, the French, the Spaniards, the Portugals, and . . ." He paused. He knew there were more, but even a big picture guy had a tough time with geography back then. "Well, without the Pope, you's alone on an island."

"You fat head! We *are* on an island. And who cares? He's King. If I was ol' King 'Enry, then I'd say, 'Who needs you's church?'"

"Then where's would you go to church?" Edward asked.

For the first time in the conversation, Henry thought. After all, the only reason he went to church at all was to keep up some pretense of piety. "Why, I see no reason Ol' King 'Enry should go to church. If I was king, I wouldn't."

While Henry may not have understood all that went into being king, it's clear that the king and he saw eye to eye on a great many things.

In a matter of a month, the town got an official declaration, by way of the bishop, making it clear that Henry had been right.

This time, it was Henry who headed over to Edward's. He had heard from James, the innkeeper, who had heard from Matthew, who happened to be at confession when Father Black, who preceded Father Young's ministry at the town parish, had received the message from the bishop. Matthew had been able, through pressing and guessing, to figure out what had been contained in the message. Now, under normal circumstances, the people involved in the conversation from here on out would have focused on why Matthew had been at confession, but this bit of news so overshadowed it that Matthew got a free pass for his sins.

Henry, not being as easily excited as Edward, walked up to the shack. Edward was on the porch, and Henry no sooner got in shouting distance when he called out, "I told ya kings don't have to worry about Popes!"

Edward quickly stood and whispered as emphatically as he could, "No need to shout your 'ead off! You want the misses to hear you. She thinks I'm off to town. You want me to get hauled out to the field to work?"

"Oh, my boy, you'd shout you's head off if you was as right as me!"

"Take a breath and tell me about it as we walk." Edward looked toward the field and judged that even if she did hear he had time for a clean getaway.

"Didn't I say that old king Henry didn't let religion shove him around none?" Henry continued.

"I recall you's saying 'who's the pope?' Rather tended near blasphemy if you ask me."

Henry didn't have time to debate about blasphemy, so he got to the point. "When the pope said, 'no divorce,' the king said, 'well then I'll start me own church.'"

Much of this was conjecture, of course. All Matthew had heard was that they were separating from the Catholics and were now The Church of England. Henry had guessed as to why.

Edward was shocked, "You mean leave the Catholics?" It was beyond comprehension. They had always been Catholic. Everybody was Catholic—and now, the king had his own church. "Where is he going to attend church? All the churches are Catholic."

"Not no more, they aint."

"What'd'ya mean?"

"The King didn't leave the Catholic church. He took all of England from the Catholic church. You's and me are now Angel-cans."

Henry thought it downright clever for the king to use angel in the name of his church when he heard it from James. "The Church of England is the church now," Henry continued.

"What about our church, and Father Black?" Edward asked.

"The church is England's."

"Is that legal?" Edward asked.

"Legal? What English court would you get to rule otherwise? And as for the priest, he's an Angel-can too," Henry continued. Henry was so proud of his king. In his mind, he was everything a king should be. He wanted to show his support and appreciation.

In his younger years, when he had dabbled in things like work, he was employed by a carpenter and had done his sign making, so he knew exactly what to do.

Edward was not so sure how he felt about no longer being a Catholic but decided that joining his friend would be more enjoyable than weeding, so off to the woods they went to find the perfect sign board.

For the next week or so, Henry worked harder than he ever had in his life, and at the end of it, he had a beautiful sign, probably the best he had ever made, that said in large text:

CHURCH OF ENGLAND
Welcome Angel Cans One and All

He and Edward marched over to the church, and with the priest not being home, took the initiative themselves and hung the sign.

It was a good thing they did because Father Black was no rebel and had been going along with the Church of England thing but had definitely not embraced it. Had Henry asked to hang the sign, he would have certainly refused. However, upon returning and seeing the sign in place, with it looking so professional and all, he assumed it had been placed by someone in authority. Even if he had known who had placed it, he lacked the energy to remove it. In fact, though it hung directly over his head for years to come, he never quite got the energy to read it in its entirety and discover that Anglicans had been misspelled.

This was the beginning of a wonderful time in Henry's life. He had always felt a closeness to his royal counterpart being that they shared a name, and this move to start his own church did nothing but further endear the king to Henry. Henry never really liked being Catholic, and he enjoyed all the news and rumors a new religion brought. Within a month, Anne Boleyn was a household name with the news of the marriage spreading faster than the plague. But what really sealed Henry's love for the king was that this upheaval of divorce, new church, and new marriage was not simply one high point of news. Many kings achieved such excitement by war or other means but usually only for a short period, but this was now a reliable pattern for King Henry. Each new trip to town came with the commotion of a new divorce, death, and remarriage. You could check the history books for how many marriages King Henry VIII actually had, but due to rumors and the same marriages being told a little differently, Henry's tally was up to twenty-two.

The only way in which King Henry VIII disappointed Henry was in the matter of his new religion. Having gone through the work of starting his own church, once he got the divorce he wanted, he forgot to finish the job and make it any better than the last church. Henry didn't like being an Angel Can any more than he liked being a Catholic. Except for his sign, he saw no difference at all between the two churches. A good portion of the village didn't even know anything had changed and that they weren't Catholic anymore, having never paused to read Henry's sign. This could be because most of them had never learned to read.

In every other way, Old King Henry was the ideal king, and no man in England mourned his death more than Henry. Edward was nothing but smiles when he learned the newly crowned king shared his name. However, over time, even Edward admitted disappointment following the lack of news generated by the new king. Perhaps they shouldn't have been too hard on King Edward. After all, he couldn't be expected to have near as many marital exploits before he hit puberty.

The only news that started from time to time were rumors that the regent, Duke Diddlehop, was working with the Archbishop of Canterbury to devise changes to the church so that being Angel Can may actually be different than being Catholic, but just when those rumors were building enough substance that they might have a chance at being true, King Edward died, and despite Duke Diddlehop doing all he could to stop it, Mary became queen and they were Catholic again.

Father Black had left the sign up, mostly because, at his age, he thought the short-lived name of King Henry's church left alone was better than the back strain it would take to remove it. But two years into Mary's reign, Father Black died and Father Young came to town. Being a young energetic priest, he removed the outdated sign. With the sign down, it seemed official: all the glories of King Henry VIII were done, and life dragged on as if he had never lived. This depressed Henry. After all, if a great king like Henry VIII could pass through and leave no ruts behind, what chance did any of us have? But a more observant man would have noticed that King Henry's reign had affected the small town of Bridgecrest because now, above Henry's shack, was a beautiful sign welcoming Angel Cans one and all to the only remaining edifice in the Church of England.

Chapter 5

The Mysterious Lady

Father Young arrived home late that night, but a day's walk had made it no clearer to him how he was going to get to know Fannie Porkshire. Having thirty years void of any interaction with the opposite sex had left him quite unprepared to accomplish the task.

Not only that, but this task was also appearing to be more difficult than he had thought. Most men get to know a woman as part of the wooing process. Yet wooing was not really what he was supposed to be doing. As he thought along the footpath, he concluded that actually wooing involved two things: one, the getting to know someone, and two, the convincing of the other party that you are worthy of their devotion. The bishop had only said he was to get to know her, this put him at a decided disadvantage from the common would-be-wooer. The two points seemed to go hand-in-hand. If you're purposely going out of your way to get to know someone, then that person will likely assume that convincing them that you are worthy of their devotion is the primary motive for such action. As far as he could see, he didn't have, or at least, should not appear to have, such a motive. He wished he had asked the bishop exactly how he should get to know her. When he had walked out of that church, the task had seemed quite simple, but the more he thought about it, the more convoluted it all appeared.

It was too late to worry about it. Father Young decided that sleep might help, so he pushed the subject out of his mind and fell asleep.

The next morning, the task did not seem any less daunting. The most obvious way to allow him the opportunity to see Fannie was to visit her. Therefore, he determined that day was as good a day as any to purchase pork and headed to the Porkshire's.

Upon arrival at "mud farms," as he had determined to call it, he saw Mr. Porkshire upon his hind legs with enough mud on him that Father figured he couldn't have been that way for long.

"Father, good to see you! I was just feeding this group of swine a unique blend of feed. This particular blend seems to be producing the most rapid growth," Mr. Porkshire said, wasting no time to begin his lecture on the appropriate methods of swinery. Father Young thought for a moment to ask if Fannie was home, but thought it might appear inappropriate for him, a priest, to be inquiring after the young lady, and he didn't want to find himself entertaining the entire family again. So, he would simply endure the lecture on pigs in hopes that Fannie might show up before too long.

This method was clearly satisfactory to Mr. Porkshire. Father Young could see Mr. Porkshire loved speaking about pigs. However, Mr. Porkshire incorrectly assumed Father Young loved hearing about them. When one must guess why something is the way it is, one might as well guess in their favor.

Occasionally during his lecture, Mr. Porkshire would ask a question to ensure his audience was managing to follow his logical but highly sophisticated discourse. But luckily for Father Young, they all followed the form of, "Isn't that right?" So, all it required Father Young to do was nod in agreement from time to time. Father Young soon found that he could tune out Mr. Porkshire entirely and focus on searching the area for Fannie if he kept a nice steady nodding motion going with his head.

Mr. Porkshire continued his work while he lectured. For two hours they went on feeding the pigs, stirring up mud, lecturing and listening before Father Young's distracted eye caught a glimpse of his angel gliding over the air towards them on the path that led to the home. Tremors in the heart began before his eyes had even relayed to the brain what they were seeing, and the jellification process started all over again.

"Oh, Father Young! What a surprise!" she said with a bright smile once close enough to the home.

If you had asked Father Young at that moment if he knew her, he would have said that the verdict was in. Her smile, her manner, the joy she brought to him, and that fair, fair face; indeed, no man could know a woman better. However, he doubted that this would meet Bishop Goldheart's criteria and tried to focus beyond the beauty so he could actually carry on a conversation with her. While his soup of a mind tried to churn away on the problem, she said, "So, what brings you our way?"

Each time she spoke, his already racing heart sped up. Her way with words left him speechless, and while he tried, he could not respond.

Mr. Porkshire was more prepared to answer the question than Father Young. "Why, Father Young has come to learn about how a wise man raises his pigs. He's a man who knows a good business when he sees it and is curious about the greatest animal the good Lord ever created."

Father Young wanted to dispute this fact, but the truth wouldn't do, so he simply nodded in agreement.

"I wouldn't be surprised if the father becomes a regular here at the farm and becomes savvy enough to buy a few pigs of his own and raise them in the church yard," Mr. Porkshire continued.

She simply smiled and said, "Well then, I will leave you two to discuss," and disappeared into the house.

Father Young tried to stop her, but it is rather hard to compose oneself when one felt more liquid than solid. His inaction left him alone in the mud with Mr. Porkshire, who smiled all the more brightly. After all, Mr. Porkshire had been happy to assume the father had come to learn of pigs, but to have it validated left him absolutely giddy.

After another hour of lecture, demonstrations and hands-on interactions with his specimens, Father Young's mind had purged all thoughts of Fannie as he was now consumed with the many reasons that he disliked pigs. He gave up hope of further interactions with Fannie and excused himself as he did his best to wipe layers of mud off his robes.

On his walk back, he wondered if the visit could have possibly been more fruitless. He was no closer to knowing Fannie than he was before his visit. Had his wooing been official, there would have been a silver lining in that he had begun to win the heart of her father, but at present, he didn't see how that was of any benefit. The other point was, he had opened the door to further visits, but what of it? All those visits could promise was getting familiar with mud, slop, snouts and hooves, not Fannie. While the plan had failed, he hadn't conceived of a better one. So, he vowed to try again the following week.

The scene just described repeated itself week after week for almost a year. Father Young would go, hoping by some miracle to be left alone with Fannie and get to talk with her. Instead, he ended up spending the day with Mr. Porkshire among oinks and squeals. No matter how fruitless these visits seemed to Father Young, he kept coming, and had to admit he still found it exhilarating to see Fannie, even if only for a few seconds. Mr. Porkshire, on the other hand, looked forward anxiously to seeing his apprentice and began to have secret hopes that Father Young would leave the cloth and take up pig farming full time. To this end, he had generously given him two pigs of his own to raise when his prized sow had its litter. Father Young had wanted to object, but Fannie had happened to walk out at this inconvenient moment turning him to a jelly again, and without realizing what had happened, he had accepted the pigs.

The pigs were nothing but a nuisance back at the parish. They were constantly breaking out of their pens and ate most of Father Young's garden. The sounds they made were not particularly conducive to sacred worship, especially during Mass when their oinks and squeals could be heard ringing throughout the chapel. Father Young had named the pigs Henry and Edward, being that these were the only common names he knew that were not biblical, biblical names being too dignified for swine. Plus, naming his pigs after the two laziest members of his parish was the only personal amusement the pigs ever brought him.

Henry was dumb, even for a pig. This particular pig spent a good portion of his life running into things at full speed. He was regularly stunned, which helped him forget how much it hurt and allowed him to do it again. Several times, Father Young had tried to give the pigs back, but Mr. Porkshire always said encouragingly, "Don't worry you'll get the hang of it." Then he would proceed to tell stories of his early days of pig farming.

When over a year had passed, Father Young had lost any hope of ever getting to know Fannie, but this did not stop his visits to the Porkshire home. They had become a habit, and they still afforded him the chance to see her smile. That smile. A man once said, "If girls realized their potential effect, they would be so careful when they smiled that they would probably abandon the practice altogether." And indeed, Father crumbled like rock amidst an explosion when she flashed her smile his way.

Just like Bishop Goldheart had found himself deeper and deeper into drink, Father Young was getting himself deeper and deeper into pig farming and mud. This unfortunate entrapment may have continued perpetually if a broken church had not caused Fannie Porkshire to fall in love.

Chapter 6

A Solemn Vow

It was a beautiful Sunday morning in March. The snow had mostly melted away, and signs of life filled the little town of Bridgecrest. Father Young was in the middle of Mass, and except for the occasional oinks from outside, things were proceeding as usual. However, as the sermon progressed, the typical noises from the pigs began to increase both in frequency and intensity. Hushed whispers began to roll through the parishioners, each speculating what could be so exciting to the pigs outside. Father Young tried, unsuccessfully, to raise his voice to compete with increasingly loud murmurs and even louder pigs. The direction from whence the noises came conveyed to him the unfortunate fact that the pigs had gotten out of the pen again, but he persisted with his clerical duties despite it. A short time later, the squeals reached their peak and there was a sudden crashing noise. Stone burst into the chapel in a poof of dust. Henry the pig had unwittingly found a deteriorating portion of the stone church and hurled himself into it. The dust settled, exposing the motionless pig among scattered stone and mortar before the startled congregation. Behind Henry remained a hole large enough to admit a donkey, but presently it was being used to admit another very excited, squealing pig, Edward, who now reveled in the accomplishment of his unconscious sibling. In the distance, a stray collie was seen retreating quickly from the tumultuous scene.

Mass was never finished that day, but Henry the pig was. The assault on the church was his last great crusade. Father Young took this as the silver lining to the whole situation. *One down, and one to go,* he thought as he chewed another bite of his pork chop that night. But the downside was rather large and manifested itself as a hole in his church. Leaving it there was not an option. It demanded quick action. Not only could it jeopardize the rest of the structure, it jeopardized the effectiveness of Sunday worship. Windows were enough of a distraction to keep most of his flock's mind elsewhere during Mass, and he knew that a hole in the church would only allow his congregation's focus to wander.

Bridgecrest was too small a town to have its own stone mason. Therefore, Father Young sent a messenger describing the problem to Bishop Goldheart. The bishop contacted members of the masonry guild who would send out a master and possibly his apprentice to fix the church.

Work must have been slow back in Lushton because even before he had heard back from the bishop, John showed up at his door. John was a young man. Handling masonry stones had clearly been a benefit to his health as his well-defined arms were difficult not to notice. His blond hair extended past the shoulders, leaving Father to wonder if he gained his strength in the same manner Samson had.

Father Young escorted the burly mason to the hole in the side wall of the church. John took one look at it and said, "This is nothing, Father, I'll have your church patched up in less than a week." Clearly, if this young mason lacked anything, it was not confidence. John's confidence helped Father Young relax and believe that the large crater in his church wall would no longer be an issue.

The next point to work out was the financial arrangement. John asked for a lump sum for the repair plus a small amount for the inn and food while he was in town to do the work. Father Young had never been party to such contracts. How to negotiate with tradesmen was not part of his seminary training. John's requests sounded reasonable to Father Young, and if it was only going to be a week, why not?

They shook on it and John got right to work clearing up the debris. Father Young went back to his quarters with a light heart.

The next morning Father Young went out to see what progress John had made. Progress had been made, but it appeared to Father Young that it was in the wrong direction. The hole was larger than it used to be. Still, Father assumed John knew his business and left him to it. Besides, today was his day to enjoy Fannie's smile. Mr. Porkshire had taken Henry the pig's death much better than Father Young had anticipated and had taken the opportunity to move his lectures on to butchering and Smoking Pork 101. Father Young had started to somewhat enjoy the class since he now had an immediate need for the information. After last week's lesson, he had gotten quite good at pork chops and was looking forward to the class on preparing bacon.

So, with both bacon and Fannie's smile on his mind, he walked rather happily towards the Porkshire's. He almost felt like skipping. In fact, he was about to take the first skip, when a singular sight took every skip he might possess out of him. It was Fannie. Usually, the sight of Fannie brought joy to Father Young, particularly when she smiled, but today, she was laughing. It wasn't the laugh that caused concern, rather it was who she was laughing with . . . John, the mason. Remove John from the scene and Father Young would have recommended it for a fresco, but with him, the whole landscape was rotten.

He continued to approach as his face involuntarily turned to a scowl. Soon both Fannie and John noticed him and turned his way.

"Good morning, Father!" Fannie said with her usual smile.

Father Young hoped his presence would cause embarrassment, but clearly, it did not. It didn't take him long to figure out why. Somehow, he had concluded that his weekly visits had impacted Fannie, or that she would somehow divine from all his talks with Mr. Porkshire how much he cared about her. But he now realized how delusional this was. After all, he was a priest and, therefore, would never mean anything to her, at least in the way he'd hoped. With all the challenges he had foreseen with his relationship with Fannie, competition with other suitors was not one he had accounted for. He had come to grips with the fact that Fannie may never be his, but his heart had not touched on the possibility that she might be someone else's. The way he saw it, another's gain only served to deepen his pain.

While wallowing in the depth of this loss, he suddenly remembered that John was supposed to be back working on his church, not perusing the local singles scene! As if anticipating his complaint, John spoke up.

"Father, the damage was a bit more than I expected so it may take a little longer, but don't you worry, I will get that church patched up. I've sent off for more stone, and hopefully it will be here in a few days." John said with a smile. "While I wait, Miss Porkshire offered to show me around your little village," turning to her and offering his arm, he added, "but I still think there is more to see. Shall we?"

"Sounds good," she said, accepting his arm.

It was the first time he saw Fannie smile that he didn't enjoy. He wanted to remind them he was there as they had seemed to forget. They headed towards town leaving Father Young to brood. Deciding he was in no mood to learn of bacon, he turned for home, but as luck would have it, Mr. Porkshire came around the corner.

"Father, glad you made it! Come with me, I was just getting ready to cut into Deloris."

The next two weeks of Mass, the chapel continued to be adorned by a gaping hole in the wall. John continued to insist the stone was on its way. Father was getting irritated with John, but what could he do? It wasn't John's fault the stone was not there, plus, he knew in all fairness, he was not a good judge of John. He was as biased a judge as could exist. John's flirtations with Fannie had not been a single occurrence. Each week, when Father Young had gone to the Porkshire's home, John had beaten him there. Father Young began to feel he was only paying John an allowance to court Fannie.

Today Father Young was bemoaning his lot in life rather than reviewing in his mind how best to prepare the hindquarters of a pig, as Mr. Porkshire had assigned him to do. As he walked back to the church from his weekly lecture, he heard banging noises coming from the church. For a moment he thought perhaps John had finally started, but quickly realized that this was impossible since he had just seen him and Fannie headed back to the Porkshire's. Getting closer, he finally made out that it was two of his congregants, Henry and Edward, hanging the "Church of England" sign back on to the church.

"I took that sign down years ago," Father yelled up at Henry.

"That you did, Father. And you was right to do so, this being a Catholic Church at the time."

"Then why are you putting it up again?" Father Young yelled. "Do you think I like taking down signs for exercise?"

A wide grin spread across Henry's face. He slowly stepped down his makeshift ladder. Father could tell that Henry was enjoying this as he walked up to him and said, "Father, I have some bad news," Henry stated, trying to sound sincere. "Our beloved Queen Mary is dead. And as you may know, pretending to be pregnant does not create babies, so she left us no heir. Therefore, Queen Elizabeth is our queen. And she has declared," he began to raise his voice for emphasis, "just like our greatest king, King Henry the Eighth, we are all Angel Cans once again!"

Father Young had no way of knowing if what Henry said was true, but he was in no mood to be toyed with. "You may very well be right, but until I get the official word, we are not going to change religions on account of some drunk wandering into town saying the queen died."

Henry put his arm around Edward and smiled as he said, "There is one more thing, Father." He paused for emphasis. "A messenger is waiting inside for you." As he finished this, he burst into laughter. Father Young was finished listening to Henry and went inside.

Inside, a page sat in a pew waiting for the priest. As he entered, the boy jumped to his feet and handed Father Young a scroll. Father Young gave the boy a coin and dismissed him.

When the Father was in seminary, there had been lots of discussion related to King Henry VIII and Edward the VI and the Church of England. He and his peers had always looked down on many of the priests at the time for not rising up with one accord and speaking out, even though it might have cost them their lives. All his friends said they would have been martyrs rather than leave the Catholic church. It was easy to look back at what had happened with Henry VIII as ancient history, something they would never have to go through now that Mary had restored them to sanity.

Standing for the Church at the cost of his life had seemed like such an easy choice when the choice didn't exist. But things had changed since then. He still loved the Church but had become aware that he and the Church did not always see eye to eye. Furthermore, what was taught in seminary and what affected real life, were two very different things. He took a quick inventory of his life and decided it wasn't that he wasn't Catholic, but he was perhaps less Catholic than he had been. Martyrdom was not the easy choice it once was. After all, were the churches really that different? When he was in seminary, the Church of England and the Catholic Church had seemed the antithesis of each other. And those who trained him under Queen Mary made sure he and his peers saw it that way. They taught him clearly that the Catholic church was all that was good and the Church of England was all that was bad.

The contrast was not as clear in the town of Bridgecrest. He had talked to those who lived through it, and here, the difference experienced by the common man was merely the presence of a new sign. And, despite his views on Henry, he had to admit he had made a decent sign. Did his day-to-day ministering among his flock really change because somewhere a king disagreed with a pope? Would he do anything any different as an Anglican priest than he did as a Catholic priest?

Why was he a priest in the first place? Becoming a priest had been so much a part of who he was for so long that it had been a long time since he sat down and took inventory. This scroll was forcing him to do just that. After three years in Bridgecrest, had he really been doing what he had planned to do? Maybe it was time for him to reconsider the priesthood altogether.

If they really were no longer part of the Catholic church, couldn't he use this as his excuse to walk away from it all? What would he do? For the first time in his life there was something else. He could have a pig farm. Mr. Porkshire would help him, and he could start his own little farm, with his own little shack, and his own little family with Fannie. He could finally be open and pursue what he really wanted, to be with her.

Years ago, he had told himself that he would give his life to God and to serving His people. Bringing people to God and the blessings of the gospel was not only a job but his purpose in life. The thought of leaving that, no matter how tempting, felt wrong. But this was a chance to recommit to something he hadn't thought about for a long time, at least not at the level he knew he should. He would stay and do what he committed to do: serve the people of Bridgecrest, as a Catholic or an Anglican. Once he made this resolve, he opened the scroll and confirmed all that Henry had said.

As he read, his resolve and recommitment left him with a feeling of peace and warmth that went from his head down to his very toes, except for his heart. It was broken. For with it came acceptance of something he always knew but was trying not to accept. Fannie would never be his.

Chapter 7

A Mason Lover

The only change Father Young had really hoped for now was that somehow John would be more motivated to fix the Church of England rather than the Catholic Church. But after a week of being in the Church of England, nothing had changed, including the hole.

It had now been over a month since the mason had come to town, and there remained no stones and no progress. Father Young was sure that whatever message was sent requesting rock either never existed, had been lost in transit, or had fallen upon the wrong ear. With nothing else to do, he decided it was time to investigate for himself.

With this in mind, Father Young headed where everyone goes in search of information: the local tavern. Father did not often enter the tavern, having little use for liquor or gossip, the only two products that seemed to flow from the establishment. Peter, an enterprising young lad who often ran messages from town to town for a small fee, sat outside the tavern, a living advertisement for his business.

"Peter, I would like to have a word with you."

"Yes, Father."

"Did John the Mason send you or someone else with a message to get some stone for the church?"

Peter thought for a moment. "Father, you know I keep my work confidential, if I talked about my customers, it'd be bad for business. But if you had something that was good for business . . ."

Father rolled his eyes and handed Peter a coin.

"Thanks Father, I'd usually charge more for this type of information, but I really hate that John guy." He tucked the coin into his purse and said, "He tried to get me to deliver the message for him."

Father Young did not like the use of that word. "What do you mean, *he tried*?"

Peter instantly began the narrative. "He comes to me and says, 'Boy, run me a message to Lushton to the head of the masonry guild telling 'em I's need one hundred full stones delivered to Bridgecrest.' To which I says, 'no problem, governor,' polite as I always am, and I gives him the price. Then he begins gettin' huffy about me price and claims that, where he comes from, boys run messages just to be neighborly. Hope you don't mind, Father, but I tells him even neighbors got to eat and I demands me fee. He says he'd show me what neighborliness is all about and shoots into the tavern to ask someone else to take his message."

"So, did he get someone?" Father interjected.

"Well, he goes in and asks some traveler, who asks him for mores money than I did. John gives him his neighborly speech. The man laughs and says, in that case, he will be neighborly, and takes the message. So, of course, mighty John comes back and give me an earful about how I's going to hell and needin' confession, and any money I's receive I should use to buy me own indulgences."

Father was not one for long narratives and only cared that the message got sent, not what John felt about Peter's eternal standing with God. Therefore, he was about to say good day to Peter, but luckily for all parties, Peter was not slow of speech, and therefore, Father couldn't get away before Peter had finished his tale.

"Then the guy who's said he'd take the message comes out and tells me what John said. He then tells me he only told John he'd do it to play him a fool, he ain't even headed to Lushton and John could go down under if he'll take a day out of his journey to be neighborly."

"And you didn't tell John?" Father Young shot back. One would think he would have been happy that his detective work paid off, but such is the risk of detective work: once we uncover the truth, all too often, it isn't really that pleasant.

Peter shifted and turned his eyes to the ground. "Well Father, what do you expect me to do? To find John so he could curse me out again? While you may not agree, Father, I really think John could use a sermon on what being the neighbourly type is."

If Father Young had been completely honest, he would have said he agreed, but didn't have time to think of the many things John needed. The more pressing problem was that he needed those stones. "Peter, do you remember the message John asked you to take?"

"Sure thing," came the quick response.

"Those stones are for the church," Father Young said, assuming that if only Peter had known this, surely, he wouldn't have been so careless about letting others know that the message had been derailed.

"I know."

So much for appealing to his Christian goodness.

"If I pay you, will you, take the message?"

"Why, Father, you know your money's as good as anyone else's. Of course, I will." Peter's business sense was bound to take him far, but for now, Father Young was just happy to see him bound for Lushton.

Within a week, a large heap of stones arrived at the church. Father Young had not told John about having to fix the message. He had planned to, but when he had seen him with Fannie, all he could muster was a brief, "Good day."

Father Young did realize that he would have to talk to John soon since the stones had arrived. It would now be incumbent on him to remind John that he was a hired mason, not Don Juan.

With this in mind, he headed off to the Porkshires. John was sitting in his usual position, with Fannie under one arm, she staring up into his golden locks. John turned to her, and he and Fannie locked eyes and sighed. Father worried a kiss was about to occur, but luckily, John then turned and looked over the muddy yard as if he was looking over the fairest meadow eyes ever saw. Then it repeated. By the time Father Young had gotten close enough for the lovebirds to notice, there had been three eye stares, three sighs, and three long looks over the muddy yard. This made three times that the father felt a certain nausea forming in his belly. John finally noticed him, "Oh Father, I'm afraid Mr. Porkshire has gone into town and will not be able to meet with you today."

Father Young maintained his composure, thinking of St. Monica, the patron saint of patience. That is, inasmuch as composure is the state one assumes when doing all one can to keep from punching another in the nose.

"I have not come to speak with Mr. Porkshire. I have come to inform you that the stones have arrived. Your work may begin."

"If that don't beat all!" he exclaimed with sheer joy. "My faith in the goodness of men was beginning to waiver. I was beginning to think that bloke who promised to take me message had allowed Satan to talk him out of it."

Father Young wanted to say, "You idiot! I had to resend your message because you didn't have the decency to pay the message boy," but somehow he couldn't quite get it out. It could be that it wasn't in his nature to scold so abruptly, but more likely it was the fact that his mind was still preoccupied with the idea of punching John's nose. He had never truly contemplated such an idea before in his life and the newness of the thought intrigued him. Quickly, he realized he knew very little about how one goes about punching noses. The mechanics of it seemed straightforward enough. Why the nose? Father was not sure but was confident that starting with the nose was standard protocol. But what does one do after they're finished with the nose? And perhaps more importantly, what does the other fellow do? John was by no means of small stature, and Father was confident he probably had more experience with noses and punching than he did.

Perhaps Father Young had more of an advantage than he thought. After all, he was a priest, and one shouldn't go around hitting priests. Then again, just because one shouldn't doesn't mean one wouldn't. Ultimately, he decided against tampering with John's nose. And simply said, "So you'll come finish the church?"

John placed a hand on his chest and took a deep breath. "Of course, Father, you know if it wasn't for those stones, I'd have already had her done and patched up weeks ago. With those stones in town, your church will be fixed faster than she crumbled." John's speech was building Father Young's faith that someday the hole may disappear. But before expectations got too high, John looked over at Fannie and finished with, "Why, first thing tomorrow, I'll be over to that church of yours."

Father Young was beginning to realize that the word "tomorrow" held a special place in this young man's heart. He had expected John to return with him today, but he was not going to drag John back. Not only that, he needed to get out of there before he allowed his emotions to rise any further and change his mind about John's nose. So, with the fortitude of Joseph running from Pharaoh's wife he said, "I look forward to it," turned, and left them to their staring and sighing.

The walk back to the church had Father Young's mind full of thoughts. One of which was how long it took to learn the art of masonry. He couldn't help but think he may be able to master the trade and patch up the church himself prior to John getting started. His mind was still somewhat frenzied when he arrived at the church and found a pageboy waiting for him. The boy handed Father a scroll, received his tip, and left. The scroll was sealed with the bishop's ring, something the bishop rarely bothered to do unless it was official business.

> *Salutations to all members of the cloth within the diocese of Lushton. Your presence is requested at the Cathedral, Saint Augustine of Hippo, on the fifth day of March, the year of our Lord fifteen hundred and fifty-eight, to discuss forthcoming events. Therefore, make necessary arrangements to attend.*
>
> *May God Bless You,*
> *Bishop Goldheart*

No doubt this had to do with the change to the Church of England, thought Father Young, already preparing his mind for a two-day-long meeting no more exciting than one of his recently attended lectures on pigs. He rolled up the scroll, and as he did, he noticed a smaller, much less official paper rolled up behind the first.

> *Father Young, I have particular things to share with you. Your dilemma may be over.*

Chapter 8

A Hopeful Bishop

Bishop Goldheart skipped through town in a manner which people were only accustomed to seeing from him after a long day at the tavern. The shock on their faces was only owing to the time of day and not to his behavior. At just after sunrise, it was far too early for Bishop Goldheart to have sufficient levels of alcohol in his bloodstream to cause such joy.

What was unknown to those confused villagers was that last night, his life had changed. For over fifteen years, his life had been hopeless, but last night, a hope had been resurrected in his mind.

It had all started on a particularly low note. The bishop got excessively drunk, even for his standards. I noted earlier that the drunker the bishop, the happier the bishop, but this pattern found an end last night. The bishop discovered that he could drink himself beyond the sensation of happiness, and in that beyond was a hopelessness that was even darker than being sober. In this state, he saw how pathetic, hopeless, and miserable his life was. This was no new revelation to the bishop, but always in times past he had simply drowned those thoughts with drink. Now, somehow, his thoughts had grown gills and seemed to survive even at great depths.

Unable to drown such thoughts, the bishop left the tavern and tried another method, distraction. In his youth, the bishop had been quite a scholar, but in recent years, he had found himself reading less and less. But tonight, to get his mind off hopelessness, he turned to reading. Just before King Edward had died, Duke Diddlehop and the Archbishop of Canterbury had sent out a book called, *The Book of Common Prayer*. It contained a message that the book was important for all bishops to read and understand. However, before Bishop Goldheart had gotten around to it, King Edward had died, the duke abjured Protestantism to save his life and the archbishop was burnt at the stake. The command to read the book fell further down the *to do* list at that point.

Bishop Goldheart was aware that with Elizabeth on the throne, they were now once again the Church of England. Of course, he had long ago stopped caring what they called the church. After all, what is in a name? A pig by any other name still stings the nostrils. Perhaps not my best analogy, maybe I should make it more positive, but you get the idea.

However, since going back to the Church of England, he had some curiosity as to what might be in *The Book of Common Prayer,* but never so much as to actually read the thing. Bishop Goldheart was not unfamiliar with religious texts. He knew that they weren't what one might call thrilling or epic. Still, he hoped it would be exciting enough to distract his mind from the emotional hangover that had already begun.

The book did not disappoint. Before he was very far in, he ran into a series of articles. The articles outlined some of the differences between the Catholic Church and the Church of England, differences that, as far as the bishop knew, had never taken effect. He read with interest as it argued against the doctrine of Transubstantiation. The idea of actually eating Christ's flesh was something he had always struggled with. As he read, he wondered if Queen Elizabeth would use these same articles. This changed how he felt about being part of the Church of England. After all, the same church that simply has a different name was not that difficult for Bishop Goldheart to accept, but it was with mixed feelings that he read on. Then he came to Article 32.

Bishops, Priests, and Deacons, are not commanded by God's Law, either to vow the estate of single life, or to abstain from marriage: therefore, it is lawful for them, as for all other Christian men, to marry at their own discretion, as they shall judge the same to serve better to godliness.

His eyes grew wide, and his heart raced. Mixed feelings no longer described how he felt. The depression that had driven him to read vanished. Instantly, visions of himself, Miss Denine, a spot of tea, a glowing fire, and a warm embrace swept over his mind. The dreams he had been fighting for years, knowing they would never be, were suddenly a possibility. The possibility of the dream made it all the more real.

With his deep depression vanishing like the morning mist before the noon day sun, the bishop suddenly realized he was very tired. Part of him wanted to read on, but his eyelids were heavy. And visions of Miss Denine were more easily viewed with closed eyes anyway. So with a large grin donning his once morose face, he embraced the vision.

Waking to sunlight pouring over him, the bishop jolted as one does after spending the night in a chair at one's desk. He was sure Miss Denine's lingering presence had been a dream, and if the book had not been opened to Article 32, he would have been convinced that it had been a dream as well. But no matter how many times he blinked, refocused, or turned pages back and forth, Article 32 still read the same.

Perhaps you have been to a restaurant, read a book, or seen a play that was so wonderful, so praiseworthy in every way, that you could not help but recommend it to others. If a stranger would stop you in the street and ask, "Which way to the local butcher?" you would politely give him directions by way of the playhouse and recommend he stop in while there. Such was how the bishop felt. He wanted to tell the world of Article 32. However, two things stopped him. One: the general populace in Lushton likely did not spend much time worrying about whether priests can wed. And two: these articles had never been officially adopted by the Church of England, and the bishop was not sure they would ever be.

Yet the bishop had hope and hope demanded action. He had joy that demanded sharing! The one group of people he knew would be eager to hear of it were his priests. His first thought was to draft a letter to the priesthood in his diocese recommending they read the *The Common Book of Prayer*; however, he was unsure how widely the book had been distributed. And even if they had the book, they may be no more obedient to the call to read it then he had originally been. He could simply send a letter with Article 32 but decided instead that he wanted to see the joy on the faces of the priests when they heard, so he began the arrangements to call a meeting.

The happy thought of being the bearer of good news made the rather mundane task of writing the invitation repeatedly go quickly and easily. It was with particular glee that he added the little note to Father Young. Like most of us, Bishop Goldheart assumed because the news made him happy, it would make everyone happy. It's difficult to assume that people see things differently than we do. But while this was an assumption about most of his priests, he had no doubt it would be good news for Father Young.

It was in this joyous state that the bishop took up the scrolls and headed into the street. Heads turned to see the smiling bishop looking so exuberant at such an early hour. Practically skipping, the bishop took off to the center of town where several boys sat hoping someone would need a messenger. Being a return customer for most of these young men, he didn't need to negotiate, and the transaction went on almost as smoothly as runners with batons.

With the message on its way, the bishop thought it was time to celebrate. As soon as the thought struck his mind, he suddenly felt a pronounced break in the steady stream of joy that had come to him since reading Article 32. To celebrate had become synonymous with alcohol, and the thought of alcohol brought with it the reality that he was all too familiar with: he was a lousy drunk. The fact had depressed him for years in a general sense, similar to how one feels knowing that, right now, somewhere, there is someone going without food. He knew it was true. He knew it was bad. However, being a lousy drunk was so overshadowed by not being with Miss Denine, it simply did not get much attention. This new hope of one day having Miss Denine dispersed the shadows of a lonely life and left him face to face with himself: the lousy drunk. The consequences were no longer general but very specific. Someone starving somewhere was suddenly himself, right here, right now.

He was a lousy drunk and Miss Denine did not deserve a lousy drunk. The habit that he had formed to cover the feelings of being without her, he realized, could ultimately be what kept him from her.

Depression had found him once again, and passersby noticed that the bishop was looking more himself. The more depressed he got, the more he wanted to drink, and the more he wanted to drink, the more depressed he got. The lines had been drawn and the war began. On one side was the desire to be the man Miss Denine deserved: sober and clean minded. On the other side stood the craving of a body very accustomed to drink.

Any general can tell you that no matter how powerful an enemy, nothing is more damaging than internal conflict, and even between his two sides there was some internal squabbling. The side that longed for the immediate drink still didn't want to see Miss Denine since she may be a rallying cry for the other side of shaping up and quitting the habit. His noble side wanted to avoid the tavern's liquid attractions, but still longed to be near Miss Denine.

Fresh off the high from his first glimmer of hope in ages, the nobler side determined that it must avoid the tavern at all costs, even if it housed the beautiful Miss Denine. Viewing Miss Denine would have to be a luxury saved for when more time and self-control sat between himself and his last drink. With that resolution, the bishop headed back to the cathedral. However, once he was at home, he had many things working against him. For one thing, there was very little to do. For years he had spent all his free time at the tavern and had forgotten what else a bishop did. Idleness allows the mind to focus squarely on what it should not. The more he thought of avoiding alcohol, the more his body wanted it. He tried to read, but compared to Article 32, the rest of his literature was dull and ill equipped to compete with thoughts of ale and beer. The second point, which his mind was repeating to him over and over again, was the fact that as a bishop, he had to regularly serve communion, and, therefore, he had an ample cache of wine.

It was with this wine that the bishop eventually succumbed to his body. The refreshing drink was wonderful and repulsive. This started a new cycle for the bishop. Before he had been sad sober and happy drunk, but today the world had flipped. He would wake each morning full of sunshine and resolve to be a new man only to become miserable again when he gave into his former addiction.

However, even while losing the fight with alcohol, he couldn't help feeling better in the mere fact that it was a fight. Fighting for something made him feel alive, more so than he had in fifteen years. The new state of happy sober and sad drunk was not a blissful life, but the bishop felt comfortable knowing that, during lucid moments, he saw a brightness in life. No longer needing to search for joy in a false reality was invigorating. All this kept the bishop fighting, even after losing battle after battle and finding himself staring at the bottom of a glass.

However, not all his battles ended in failure, and by the time the day arrived for the priests to assemble, he had not touched "the stuff" in two days. And while two days may seem like a short time, any alcoholic will attest those two days represent hundreds of battles fought and won.

He was proud to be sober for the priests; however, he was not glad to have the meeting. When he had called the meeting, he was exuberant to share with his brothers the joy he had discovered in the *Common Book of Prayer,* but now in the midst of internal warfare, he did not feel like entertaining a host of celibate old men. The bishop also wondered if he was wise to share the information at all. Who was he to say Queen Elizabeth was even going to adopt the articles as her own? He may inflate the hopes of all these men only to find they can't marry at all. Perhaps one should not brandish the subject of ending a man's required celibacy too lightly. This point had been repeated to him a thousand times by his darker side. In fact, while his darker side seemed to be a mighty warrior when it came to brute force, its vocabulary was very small. It consisted of, "This might all be a waste," and, "Let's go get a drink."

Even with its lack of eloquence, the darker side did have a point. There was no guarantee he would ever be allowed to marry Miss Denine or anyone else. It was this point that made up his mind to focus on every article except 32. Originally, he couldn't wait to see the faces of the excited priests when they were told that marriage was indeed an option, but that joy had been tempered by reality. After all, his diocese already had a brokenhearted bishop and a priest with a crush. Further love entanglements would not make his life, or anyone else's, any easier. The focus of the meeting would be the change in Mass and other less exciting articles, skipping entirely over Article 32.

Not long after the bishop had settled on this approach, the doors to the church opened. One by one, the priests entered the Cathedral. Gatherings such as this were infrequent, and the priests enjoyed the chance to speak with one another. These birds of a feather rarely had opportunities to be a flock. Being the only educated men in their small towns meant that they often felt isolated. Also, being a priest comes with a certain expectation of piety. This expectation among their congregations left an intense pressure. These gatherings allowed them to relax, feeling that the father next to them was more understanding than judgmental. A trained observer would have noticed that each man's robes had a more relaxed fit.

Even when all were present and accounted for, there was no rush to begin the meeting. Father Baker was in the middle of telling several other priests about his most recent exorcism. Father Hampton was telling another smaller group about how he had found a merchant who delivered pomegranates, and he purchased sufficient to produce a pomegranate pie. In a testament to what most interested the priests, several who were listening to the exorcism story moved over to listen to Father Hampton when the word pie wafted through the air.

Father Young had thought of little else besides the bishop's cryptic letter since it had come. The entire walk to the village, he wondered what "solution" to what "dilemma" it could be? The obvious was, of course, the issue with Fannie. But how the bishop could solve a love entanglement such as his, he could not fathom. *Perhaps he has heard of the hole in the chapel wall*, he thought. If that were the case, he hoped the bishop had also heard about John and that perhaps "dilemma" was John's fitting surname.

Father Young had planned on asking the bishop first thing when he arrived what the note meant. However, upon Father Young's entrance, the several groups, even those speaking about pomegranate pie, stopped talking and turned to him. The father was not sure if the bishop knew of the continuing saga of the hole, but after five seconds in the church, he was made aware that every other priest did. He was met with a barrage of questions and conjectures.

"Is it true burglars busted into your church?"

"No, I heard a wild boar smashed it."

"I heard a desperate lover rammed into it attempting to take his life."

Father Young was not prepared for the interrogation and was not sure how much of the story he wished to share, so he took the easy way out. "It was a wild boar." Just because a pig is domesticated does not mean he is not wild, and Henry the pig was the not so living proof of that fact.

Father Young hoped this would end the conversation so he could speak to the bishop, but like all good investigators, these priests wanted details. He soon realized that his conversation with the bishop would have to wait, so he sat down and indulged his anxious audience.

The bishop, much like his audience, was in no rush to begin, but having placed himself on the chancel, he had isolated himself from the conversation. Time goes much slower from the perspective of the one watching the conversation when compared to those participating. He knew his lack of preparation was not going to change just by idly watching this social commotion, so before those below him were finished with their conversations, he rose and brought the brethren to attention.

The opening was not too exciting, but he needed to give them some idea of why they had been summoned. To the best of his ability, he gave a rundown of the history from Henry VIII to the present. This may sound simple enough, but what is now history was then recent events. Time seems to clarify these events and allows us to see some as facts, and some as fiction, or at least to decide we know as much. But time had not yet had enough of itself to clear the fog. The events were filtered and mixed with rumor and conjecture. Not only that, but he had to give the story from the perspective of a bishop who had been asked to change loyalties several times in the last years. Despite these difficult waters, he swam well and came at last to the *Common Book of Prayer*. He did, however, neglect to mention why it had taken him over seven years to read it.

This had all built to the expected climax where he would state that the book was now being adopted under the rule of Queen Elizabeth.

Therefore, when he said, "We have come together today to discuss these changes to *prepare for a time* when they *may possibly* be implemented," there was notable disappointment in the room. The audience was prepared for a change, they were amped up for change, not for a future change, a proposed change, or worst of all, a possible change. An important sounding summons, a special meeting, and a long walk or carriage ride had prepared them. They wanted change. We all want change. Even if we hate change, we look forward to it. It gives us something to complain about. A more raucous crowd of less decorum may have gone for pitchforks, but the priests being the pacifists that they were, did not yell, complain, or even throw broccoli. Instead, they proclaimed in their minds that the meeting was officially "boring," nestled into their pews, and prepared for a long nap.

It is never fun to address an audience as responsive as cauliflower, but this had its plus side. The bishop had not done much by means of preparation. His intentions to read over the articles again and to read beyond Article 32 before the meeting were not actually fulfilled. The two days of victorious sobriety were only achieved by keeping his mind and body occupied, and reading was not sufficient to the task.

Therefore, Bishop Goldheart had determined to simply read the book and discuss each article. As noted earlier, he intended to skip Article 32, however, the first thirty-one articles had so sufficiently sedated the audience, that the bishop was fairly sure that if he had said that Article 32 was requiring mandatory castration among the clergy, he would have received no more than a yawn or two. Therefore, the bishop plowed ahead to Article 32.

Little things twist fate. Perhaps this is what makes fate so fickle. In our case, it was a fly and a small one at that. This fly had found a particular liking to one of the large coarse white hairs protruding from Father Monagol's ear and decided to use it as a perch on which to rest. Father Monagol was a large senior priest having reached the ripe old age of 53. He had determined to use the bishop's speech to gain some not much needed rest. At first, he had found the pews a bit hard for a doze, but finally managed the task at around Article 12. However, it was just as Article 32 was about to be read that the fly made contact with the inner workings of his ear. This was not enough to wake the father—a twenty-article sleep can be quite deep—but it did cause the priest to jolt a bit. In turn his jolting elbow hit Father Woodward, who having only fallen asleep at Article 28, woke up. This resulted in having one conscious priest hear the bishop state:

> *Bishops, Priests, and Deacons, are not commanded by God's Law, either to vow the estate of single life, or to abstain from marriage: therefore, it is lawful for them, as for all other Christian men, to marry at their own discretion, as they shall judge the same to serve better to godliness.*

Words can be a powerful motivator of men, and these caused Father Woodward to jolt with even more vigor than a fly could evoke, causing priests on both sides of Father Woodward to awaken. This was particularly impressive given that the priest to his left had been asleep since Article 2. Now there were two more priests awake to hear Father Woodward blurt out, "Did you just say we can marry?"

Now both priests who had just awakened jolted in turn, awakening their neighbors, and promptly relayed to them, "Bishop says we can marry!"

The jolting passed through the congregation like a pig running through a church. Soon every priest was awake and talking about Article 32—that is, every priest except Father Young. He had far too much on his mind to talk.

Chapter 9

A Suffering Pig

Father Young was back on the road, a day's journey ahead of him to think over the news and then think through it again. While there is much to be said for faster modes of transportation, it does limit time to think. Among the ruckus of jolting priests during yesterday's meeting, Father Young thought for a moment that he was now permitted to marry. At that moment, Father Young closed his eyes, and the priests disappeared. He was holding Fannie's hand, asking her to accept his, forever. But happiness faded quickly. He saw Fannie's face, it wasn't happy. Before she could reply, the bishop had pulled him from his dream. The bishop calmed the crowd and reminded the brethren that these changes may or may not occur. The intensity of the news had led them to temporarily forget that this news was not a guarantee.

Father Young trudged on, and heavy raindrops began falling, further dampening his mood. No one in the congregation was more affected than Father Young. For a brief moment, he thought he could marry his Fannie, but what stood out in his mind was that this did not end as a happy moment. He feared more than looked forward to what Fannie would say if he ever did get the chance to ask her. He was disappointed—disappointed that he had so miserably failed to get to know Fannie. For at that moment, popes and vows didn't keep him from Fannie, rather it was his own inability to woo the opposite sex.

Once the bishop reminded everyone that this was only to prepare them in case these changes did take place, Father Young was relieved. "Prepare" was the word that stuck out in his mind. Whether or not he could ever marry may be out of his control, but he could at least be prepared if that day ever came.

With all this came new resolve to get to know Miss Fannie Porkshire. The one fact Father Young could not deny was that the greatest stumbling block to his mission was John, the very man he had invited to town. If Fannie Porkshire were to ever become Mrs. Fannie Young, someone would have to do something about John, and Father Young still had most of a day's journey to figure out what. He kicked at a rock in the road, imagining it was a certain stone mason. He needed a plan.

Within five seconds of arriving at the church, Father Young knew plan A wouldn't work. Plan A held the prominent spot as the first plan because it was the easiest. It was the "do nothing" plan. The plan involved hoping that while he had been gone for several days, John had patched the church and was ready to move on. But alas, the hole was no more patched up than it was when he had left; in fact, a few more stones lay as rubble on the floor. These stones, had decided while he was gone that they were Catholic and, therefore, were unfit to remain attached to a structure that was now the Church of England. There they lay on the floor, an anthem to John's progress.

Father Young was prepared to move on to plan B, and surely would have done so, if it were not for the cries of pain that emanated from behind the church. Around back, Father found Edward the pig lying on the ground, looking bloated and in extreme pain. Father had not paid much attention to Edward once Henry had died. Besides throwing food out a couple of times a day, he hardly knew Edward was still alive. On occasion, he made a brief mental note that Edward had grown quiet since Henry, the pig, had passed, but he rationalized that with no one to oink and squeal at, the pig just stopped. Now the pig squealed louder and more intensely than Father had ever heard. He wanted to put plan B into action, but as much as he did not exactly love Edward, he could not stand to see him in this much pain. He knew he had better get Mr. Porkshire to help him do whatever it is you do to help swelling swine.

Despite being tired from his long journey, Father Young immediately set out for the Porkshire home. Mr. Porkshire was happy to help when Father Young arrived and explained the situation. Nothing could outweigh the importance of a swine in distress, so he dropped everything to come right away. Father Young had expected to see John and Fannie welded together on the porch, so as they started for the church Father Young asked if the love birds were about. Mr. Porkshire's demeanor changed and said, "They don't spend much time at the home anymore." Then with obvious desire to change the subject said, "Tell me again what was going on with your pig."

"It was moaning and squealing very loudly," stated Father Young.

"Was it a deep throat squeal or high squeal?"

Father Young had never thought of classifying pig squeals but thought he better play along, "I'd say deep."

"That's a good sign," Mr. Porkshire half muttered to himself as he thought. "Was it short rapid squeals or more drawn out?" he asked.

Father Young had no idea but knew it might offend Mr. Porkshire if he admitted to not taking notes about the squeals prior to his coming over and asking for help. No doubt there was no greater expert than Mr. Porkshire when it came to pig squeals. So, putting his best guess forward, Father Young said, "It was more drawn out than not."

"Also, good. Could you make the sound?" Mr. Porkshire continued as he turned his head, prepared to listen and diagnose as they walked.

This was beyond Father Young's abilities, and he simply said, "I don't think I could do it justice."

"That's okay," assured Mr. Porkshire "You'll learn with time. Was it like this?" Mr. Porkshire went on to make the most horrid noise Father Young had ever heard a human produce, but he had to admit that it sounded like a pig.

"No, that's not quite it."

"Like this then . . ."

Mr. Porkshire went on making various well-rehearsed sounds of swine as Father Young tried to state how well they resembled Edward until they were within a hundred yards, and they could hear the real thing in the distance. Mr. Porkshire stopped, listened, began to smile, and then with a look of pure joy, shook Father's hand and said, "Congratulations, my boy! Congratulations!" Then he took off running towards the church.

The last ten seconds left Father Young completely stunned. First, he had no idea why Mr. Porkshire had congratulated him; second, he had not been called, "my boy," in over fifteen years. But mostly, he never imagined someone as large as Mr. Porkshire would perform so well in a hundred-yard dash.

By the time Father Young arrived at the church, Mr. Porkshire had created a bed of straw, guided Edward onto it, and was rubbing the pig in a very odd fashion. Noticing the father, Mr. Porkshire explained, "We want her to be as comfortable as possible."

This surprised Father Young. The possibility of Edward the pig being female had never occurred to him. Mr. Porkshire had not yet given a lecture on determining the sex of pigs, or if he had, it was among the many Father Young did not pay attention to. Father Young had just assumed his were male. He didn't know why. Just the way his pigs acted seemed very male to him. He now realized that no pig he knew had much femininity and yet some of them had to be female, and Mr. Porkshire, who was one to know, felt that Edward was among them.

"So, what's wrong with her?" Father Young asked.

"Nothing's wrong with her," stated Mr. Porkshire. "She's . . ." he was about to say something when Edward or should we say Edwina, let off a squeal louder than before and began to convulse almost as if her entire body were tightening. What occurred next was not pleasant and details will not be given, but blood and several other bodily fluids all played their parts, and then Mr. Porkshire said, "Here it comes!", out popped a tiny snout. Mr. Porkshire smiled with pride, while Father Young teetered with nausea. In short order, Mr. Porkshire held a piglet in his arms. Father Young had always been amazed at how casually Mr. Porkshire handled mud, but dealing with mud was nothing compared to what this piglet was covered with, and Mr. Porkshire seemed to mind it even less. He took it to a water basin and cleaned it off before laying it next to his mother. Father Young couldn't believe it, three months ago Henry the pig had died, and he was happy to be down to one pig. Now pigs were popping up in his yard. When Henry the pig came crashing through the church, Father Young was sure Henry was done interfering in his life, but clearly, he was not. Henry had left more than just a damaged wall as his legacy.

The scene of squeals, blood, and popping snouts was repeated eight times throughout the night, and by the time Mr. Porkshire had placed number eight next to Edwina, the sun had risen. The ordeal was all so intense. Father Young had assumed it had taken place in an hour or two, not the ten that had transpired. Watching this miracle unfold had kept Father Young awake, but now that it was over and the pigs lay peacefully nursing off their mother, he realized how incredibly tired he was.

"Seeing all this just invigorates you, doesn't it?" Mr. Porkshire said as he jumped up. Clearly when it came to his desire for night caps, Father Young was alone.

"Thank you for your help, Mr. Porkshire. I would have been lost without you," said Father Young.

"I wish I'd known she was pregnant! I would have given you birthing lessons!" Mr. Porkshire said, clearly sorrowful for the lost opportunity. "But don't be too sad. I have a litter coming soon, so it will give you a chance to learn to birth soon enough." Father Young did not look forward to the opportunity.

"But now that it's over, I was wondering if you might help me with a little matter?" Mr. Porkshire continued.

Father Young felt that if it was anything but garnishing a pillow with his head, he would be of little help. Yet, when a man has brought eight healthy swine into the world for you, what can you say? "Of course, I would be glad to help."

"See, Father, I've been meaning to talk to you. You being my priest and all. I'm in a bit of a sticky spot and I'd like your advice. It's about Fannie—she wants to get married."

Married! Father Young couldn't believe it. How could she? In an instant he saw his only goal in life fading away. He felt his joy and happiness slip right through his hands, just when he was on the verge of grasping it. No matter how far we truly are from our goals, once they fall out of reach, we tend to feel they were within our fingertips. He sat down on a rock, head in hands.

All the images of him growing old with Fannie and their children disappeared. Now he was going to grow old with Edwina and the eight little porkers. Mr. Porkshire looked up at Father. "I felt the same when I heard. She seems awfully young. But lookin' back, I was her age when Mrs. Porkshire and I decided to marry. No, it is not her age that bothers me. I worry about John."

Father Young couldn't have put it better. Of all the things to worry about in this life, John had to top the list.

"Father, I heard them talking on the porch, and they spoke of marriage. I didn't mind having him around before, but after I overheard that, I've given him the cold shoulder. He must have noticed because I see less and less of him and Fannie. I believe the next time I see his face he'll be asking me for her hand."

This story was doing little to elevate Father Young's mood, but the more Mr. Porkshire spoke, the more confused Father Young became as to what he wanted him to advise about the situation. After all, if you plan to hire someone to sneak up on an individual in a dark alley and bop him on the head, you usually don't start by contacting the local priest.

"Well, when he comes, I want to be prepared with what to say. I'm at a loss, for on one hand, I'm no duke. Who am I to refuse a fellow working man my daughter's hand?"

Father Young felt it was fairly liberal of Mr. Porkshire to be calling John a working man but decided not to point it out.

"But on the other hand," Mr. Porkshire continued, "John has been by my home a hundred times, and I don't think he has once smiled at my beautiful swine. To be surrounded by the beauty of pigs and never notice makes me worry if he is of a sound mind. Father, I hate to judge another man, but I believe John doesn't even like pigs. I'd go so far as to say, he might even dislike them."

The gavel had dropped, the verdict was in. Father Young could have given a much more expansive list of John's weaknesses, but none would hold much weight in the courtroom of Mr. Porkshire's mind. To be found guilty of the dislike of swine was the ultimate offense. They had different reasons, but Father Young and Mr. Porkshire saw eye to eye on John. Now Father Young was actually enjoying the conversation, and prepared to jump in.

"How can I help?"

"Well, Father, I would like to say 'no' when he asks."

Father Young was glad to hear this and felt that immediate reinforcement was necessary.

"I think that is wise."

Mr. Porkshire was glad to see Father was on his side and continued.

"What I worry about is this isn't 1200 anymore. Then, a father's word was law. We live in this darn modern age when girls hear fairy tales of women who marry whomever they want! When Papa says no, they ride off into the sunset with their poorly chosen anyway. I have no dowry to offer that might persuade her to listen to her father. How can I say, 'no' in such a way that she'll listen, in such a way that she'll see I want the best for her? I know you're not a father, Father." He paused, processed what he just said, and moved on. "But you are learned in books and speaking, what should I say to her?"

Now Father Young was at a loss. What does one say when given the chance to stop the marriage of the woman they love to someone else? He was more anxious for Mr. Porkshire to succeed than Mr. Porkshire himself, but sometimes, wanting something too much doesn't make us wise in what we say. So, what finally came out was not the well-scripted words of a learned man but simply, "Tell her she can't."

Mr. Porkshire pulled his head back, and Father Young instantly felt that his advice was wrong, "No, encourage her but leave it up to her. She's a good girl, she'll listen, and do what's right." The words hurt, he worried this would only lead to him being on the wrong side of the altar at a wedding, but he knew it was the right thing.

"You are wise for one who has never had children, I should trust her." He looked down at the piglets as they nursed. "It is hard for any parent to see their child as much older than this sow sees these little ones. They are so perfect but need so much protection. Part of what makes it so hard is I see so much of myself in Fannie. But you don't want to hear about this . . ."

"I'm happy to listen," significantly understating his desire.

That was enough and Mr. Porkshire continued, "Fannie is stubborn. Just like me. Truth is I remember going to my father when I was Fannie's age. I had met the most beautiful woman. The Missus fascinated me as much as the twirl in a pig's tail."

Father Young wasn't sure this was the most romantic analogy but could sense how much the thought meant to him.

"My pa didn't approve. She had been raised in circumstances a bit above us Porkshires and my father thought going after her would only bring embarrassment to her, our family, and ultimately, if I could do the impossible and get her to marry me, that I would spend my days trying to make her happy and failing. I didn't care. I wanted her, and fighting for her, winning her over, and making her happy is my greatest accomplishment in my life."

Father Young couldn't believe it. Mr. Porkshire didn't see his pigs as his greatest accomplishment. The thought was almost unconscionable and left the father's broken heart further aching. He had never met or assumed he would never meet someone who loved their career more than Mr. Porkshire, yet Mr. Porkshire knew that Mrs. Porkshire was first. Was he giving up the most important fight he would ever have in his life?

While the father's thoughts circled, Mr. Porkshire continued. "Well hopefully I'll get a chance to talk to her. We don't have much time left for sleep—we better get some. I'll be back tomorrow to check on the piglets." Mr. Porkshire rose and began to walk back towards his home.

Father Young watched the man whom he had spent so much time with over the last year of his life as he walked away and realized for the first time that he had much more to learn from this pig farmer. It was time for him to fight, and it all began with Plan B.

Chapter 10

A Sorrowful Goodbye

Sun through the window awoke Father Young. He couldn't say for certain exactly where he was, on account of the bright light. Soon enough, he realized he was in his own room, but couldn't account for the fact that he was waking in what appeared to be the late afternoon. Just then the squealing of eight little pigs came through his permanently opened window and his late night with Mr. Porkshire came to mind. The thought of raising eight pigs was depressing to Father Young, but as overwhelming a task as it was, he knew it was not task number one. First, he must deal with John.

Father Young was not sure of the proper way to fire people, but step one was to contact the guild and request a new mason. "Would they think it an odd request if I asked for an aged man?" he thought. Odd or not, he thought it worth a try. Many countries have thrown out a dictator only to welcome a tyrant. Father Young had no desire to say goodbye to John and say hello to Hercules.

It was with this action in mind that he thrust open his door only to find a rather startled John on the other side of it. He had known that a face-to-face with John might need to take place, but "might" stood out as the dominant part of that sentence. Also, it was in the future. Like an eight-year-old at his first catechism, the babbling began instantly. "John, oh . . . I see you . . . are here. I uh . . . guess you walked," he said trailing off.

Luckily, John came to his rescue. "Father, I have some bad news."

Father Young had planned to be the one bearing bad news to John, but John was prepared, Father Young was not, so John continued. "I will be unable to finish your church." Even a priest can be taken by surprise by the mercy of God at times. Father was thinking that this was just such a time. John continued. "I have to go to Lushton for some other assignments."

Father had oft used the line, "That your burdens may be light," but only now did he understand what it meant. His feet were lifting off the floor even as John continued, "I will send someone else to finish."

Father Young should have done more to hide his elated state, but a child having just discovered sugar would scarcely have been so animated. So it was with glee that Father asked John, "Do you know who you might send?"

John was visibly offended by the obvious joy that Father experienced when hearing of his future absence. "I am not sure, but most likely it will be George."

"How old is George?" shot back Father Young. The image of Hercules riding into town had not escaped his mind.

"I never asked George how many years he has been frolicking about on this earth."

John's attitude wasn't any better than his work ethic. But Father needed to know and what he was searching for wasn't a number, "Is George old?"

John paused, "I'd say George hath borne himself beyond the promise of his age." John smiled, clearly finding his tongue a good messenger of his cleverness.

"You do know George, don't you?" Father Young got out.

"Sure, I know George."

"So, is he older than me?" Father Young said, hoping the reference would help clear John's mind from whatever riddles he was playing with.

John took a hard look at Father Young as if looking over him for the first time. It was no mystery to Father Young what he was thinking. He was used to people seeing the robe and not the man. And just as to him all pigs were male, so too many saw all priests as old no matter their age. John was figuring out as he looked at the father truly for the first time that Father Young was not an injustice to his name. "I'd say George is definitely older than you."

This was reassuring to Father Young and what was more reassuring was the ease with which it was answered. Father accepted that his lack of hemming and hawing meant that George was old enough to ensure he would be no foe.

"Well John, thank you for your help." The comment almost came off as sarcastic, but it was sincere. Father Young could speak as one who now saw John no longer as a problem but a past problem, and a past problem, if endured, brings fondness. Father Young never thought that he'd be fond of John, but here he was so happy to see him gone, that he could feel some warmth in his heart for this former foe.

"Help?" John lifted one eyebrow, "Oh yeah happy to a . . . help. Well, good day, Father," he said, and turned and headed towards Lushton.

Father Young basked in the moment, mentally capturing the picture of John walking down the dusty path. John had entered Father Young's view hundreds of times over the past month; but this was definitely the view he liked most. Enjoying the moment could have gone on for days, but he understood that while his quest had taken a turn for the better, it was far from over. Pulling himself back to the task at hand, he took the next step, and that step was in the direction of the Porkshire's.

Within a hundred yards of the Porkshire's, Father Young knew something was wrong. Peter, the message boy, was leaving the home. An official message to a resident was extremely rare, but this was not the only clue that raised Father Young's suspicions. Inside the cottage, someone was crying—one could even say wailing. Peter shuffled away, clearly anxious to have that delivery over. Father Young listened, assuming it must be Mrs. Porkshire—either that or Mr. Porkshire was an incredible tenor. Peter quickly passed by, leaving Father Young and the wailing at the porch. Father Young turned to knock but suddenly realized that he did not know the etiquette in such matters. Does one knock, obviously interrupting the wailing? Pleading ignorance wouldn't work given the volume of the wail. So, frozen between knocking and walking away, Father Young stood there until Mr. Porkshire opened the door. This did not improve the awkwardness of the situation for Father Young. When the door opened, he was leaning towards leaving, but he now attempted to play the part of a deaf man who had just arrived.

Pretending just to have arrived and not to have heard the wailing was hard enough that it left Father Young stuttering. Luckily, Mr. Porkshire wasn't interested in how long Father Young had been on the porch. He was, instead, happy to see him.

"We better let the Missus be," he said in a whisper and motioned Father Young to follow as they walked in the direction most men walk in relation to a woman's cries. When they could safely talk without Mrs. Porkshire either hearing or drowning them out, Mr. Porkshire spoke, "It's Fannie . . . She's left."

"Left to town?" Father Young asked.

"Yes," Mr. Porkshire said, not missing a step, "but not our town."

"So, she'll be back tomorrow?" questioned Father Young.

Father Young instantly began the mourning process which started with denial.

Handling a hysterical wife was difficult enough, but Mr. Porkshire was not prepared to deal with an oblivious priest. So, he tried to make it clear, "No, my wife was crying because Fannie is left and is not planning on coming back."

It began to settle in . . . and Father Young did not like it. "But . . . where has she gone to?" The crisis was serious, so serious in fact that in his flurry of mind, he had ended his sentence with a preposition.

Mr. Porkshire was not one to let grammar slow a conversation. "Couldn't say for sure. She asked Peter to tell us she needed to get away and would not be coming home for a time." Mr. Porkshire was handling the whole situation marvelously. Father Young, on the other hand, thought Mrs. Porkshire had chosen the more reasonable course of action.

Tears were beginning to show in Father Young's eyes. Mr. Porkshire chose to ignore it and continued his narrative, "It was good of her to tell us, and it was good of Peter to deliver the message, which he did for free. He made that very clear. Father, do you remember what I spoke to you about earlier?" Mr. Porkshire continued.

Father Young was in a strange daze. All he could think of was that he had been so happy to see John leave and it was all for naught. Fannie was gone as well. With this going through his mind, it took a while before he realized the question had been sent his way.

Mr. Porkshire noticed the father was unprepared to answer and helped him out. "When I asked you about what you thought about John and Fannie."

"Oh, yes I do recall that's what we spoke about." Father Young's fuzzy brain continued, as did the prepositions.

"Well, I had a chance to talk to her. I went into it, planning as we discussed to just give advice and leave it to her. And I did not forbid her from marrying John but told her that if she did, then I had pigs smarter than my daughter. I probably took it a bit far. I even stated that I did not think John liked pigs. Indeed, it was at that moment that things got a bit animated. And before I continue, Father, I want you to realize that Fannie was upset and should not be judged too harshly on what she said. Even as horrible as what she said is, I suppose she should be forgiven." Mr. Porkshire became very sincere as this went on, pausing with considerable pain in his voice as he showed the first sign of weakness Father Young had ever seen the great pig farmer display.

"She said . . . she said . . ." Tears began to well up in his eyes. "She said she hated pigs." Father Young could see that Mr. Porkshire was glad to have it out and over with. He quickly composed himself and his matter-of-fact delivery returned. "No doubt she was upset with me. I assume she's gone to see her aunt. It is the only other place she knows. While it brings me no joy to be without her, I see no harm in her going to see her aunt as long as she not only left us behind, but that she left John as well."

This last line made Father Young realize that John's sudden dislike for keeping up the pretense that he would one day fix the church, the wailing of Mrs. Porkshire, and Fannie's quick exit were all linked together in some horrid plot. This put Father Young in a poor position. In a world ruled by gossip, Father Young had rarely participated. He had always had little reason to, nor did he have much access to it for that matter. But his duty in this situation was obviously to play the part of an informer. Realizing that his news was not going to be received well, he paused and asked himself how best to deliver what might be a crushing blow. "Mr. Porkshire, I saw John earlier today."

"Good. Glad the scoundrel is still around," Mr. Porkshire said.

"John informed me that he was leaving town and heading to Lushton for work," Father Young slowly got out and then added, "He was headed that way when I last saw him."

"What!?" yelled Mr. Porkshire, his face turning a bloated crimson reminiscent of Edwina just before pushing out her piglets.

Father Young, having been the deliverer of the news, felt it was somehow his fault. This led his mind to scramble and try to figure out how to calm Mr. Porkshire. Father Young's mind was not as fast as Mr. Porkshire's tongue.

"That scoundrel, that hustler, that reprobate, that . . ." A man once made note that the English language is chock-full of slanders to be used on females who choose to engage in intimate relations before the proper time but is noticeably short on such terms for their male counterparts. But where the English language fell short, Mr. Porkshire's imagination excelled. It was during this rant that Father Young suddenly realized the gravity of the situation. His mind was so focused on how to bear the news to Mr. Porkshire that he had failed to internalize the news himself. It was only as Mr. Porkshire's insults got more colorful when Father Young realized what might be going on. Fannie and John had eloped.

Father Young thought of how joyous he had been to see John walking away, never knowing that while he was departing their town, he was taking with him Father Young's greatest treasure. Amid the darkness of his mind, all he could think of was that it was over. He had lost his Fannie.

Chapter 11

The Discovery

Mr. Porkshire was not one to concede quickly. If Fannie was going to elope, it would not be without him giving his all to stop it. Anger had turned into a resolute determination to act. "Father Young, I have a proposition for you. Join me in a rather brisk walk to Lushton or be so kind as to inform my wife that I won't be home for supper."

Father Young was not the decisive man that Mr. Porkshire was and, therefore, it speaks of his deep love for Fannie that, with only several moments of hesitation, he was briskly following in Mr. Porkshire's footsteps.

Their journey had begun hours after John's, which meant that they would arrive several hours after him, no matter how brisk their pace. Father Young would have liked to speak more with Mr. Porkshire, but their pace could not afford any oxygen for speaking.

But while words were impossible, thought was not. This journey was to be a test of Father Young's love. Indeed, pushing a man who did not care for long physical exercise into hours of strenuous exertion is a steep test indeed. The fact that Father kept up with the steady march of the pig farmer would be proof enough for anyone that Father's love was true. But the physical test was not the only one to conquer. Mentally, he was struggling with the question of whether Fannie even deserved his love. After all, he was a priest. Even if he could marry, would he want a woman who was willing to defy mother and father and elope with a long haired, lazy mason? What of her judgment?

The simple problem boiled down to this new question. Assuming Mr. Porkshire led a successful march to Lushton ending in victory with Fannie's hand still intact, would Father Young still want that hand? For hours he grappled over it, going back and forth in his mind. However, when he finally allowed his mind to imagine once more, as he had often done before, that impossible moment where she fell as much in love with him as he had been with her, he knew it was still his greatest hope. He realized the deep offense he was feeling for her actions had been born of jealousy and dashed hopes, not by the follies of youthful romance and rebellion. He knew he would have happily overlooked such folly had those youthful whims been directed at him instead of John. Certainly, if the hand was ever offered to him, he would have little consideration for its former choices, but would consider that moment the most gracious and joyous choice ever made on his behalf and would gladly accept it.

With renewed clarity and determination, his mind began to focus on the task at hand. Thoughts and worries turned to desperate prayer that it would not be too late. With the focus of a goal, the aches and pains that were steadily on the increase took a back seat. Father Young now understood why Mr. Porkshire was able to tread on despite his excess girth. He was inspired by a higher cause. When plagued by doubts and crushed dreams, it was grueling. Now it was exhilarating. Father Young conjectured that marching with William of Orange would have scarcely been so exciting.

With each step, the mission seemed to grow in importance. The emotional build up was so great that Mr. Porkshire and Father Young felt that they may have been able to lay siege on all of Lushton, never mind a single love-struck mason.

As they burst into town ready for victory, they both suddenly realized they had a small problem. If they had desired to lay siege on the entire town, it would have been rather simple to figure out where to begin. Anywhere would do. But while their much smaller target made for smaller overall work, it also left the task of locating the target. So, there they stood huffing, having made a valiant final charge just before town. Mr. Porkshire could only hope that John would have a firework show to celebrate their proposed elopement, and now would be a great time for it to start.

They looked around from where they stood, but no explosion or lightshow was forthcoming. So, in a rather anticlimactic move, they turned and headed towards the tavern.

The tavern was always the default location for travelers. It was the center for both action and gossip in town. Father Young thought it rather unlikely John and Fannie would be there, but someone there might know their whereabouts.

Upon entering the tavern, there was nothing out of the ordinary. A few travelers sat eating and drinking. The beautiful Miss Denine stood behind the bar pouring a beer. The only local was Bishop Goldheart, in his usual seat, staring at Miss Denine. Father Young had no idea where to go, who to approach, or what to do, but Mr. Porkshire did not share his dilemma and headed straight for the bar.

"Elizabeth," he said warmly, addressing Miss Denine.

"George, I know why you're here and you might as well turn yourself around and go back to your pigs." she said sternly.

Father Young quickly tried to connect how Mr. Porkshire and Miss Denine may have known one another, but nothing came to mind.

"So, I take it Fannie's here then," Mr. Porkshire said rather hotly.

This George was full of all sorts of tricks, thought Father Young. Not only did he know Miss Denine, he could also tell that she was harboring Fannie with hardly a word on the subject. Father Young was lost indeed but was gaining faith in his leader.

"I won't be lyin' to you," said Miss Denine. "But she doesn't want to see you, and as long as I'm breathin', she won't have to."

"I'm her father," he shot back.

"And I don't care," she snapped. Years of running a tavern had left her sharper and more brash than most. Her quickness caught Mr. Porkshire off guard, and while it took him a minute to formulate a comeback, he wasn't backing down.

"You, of all people, should care enough for Fannie to stop her from such destructive behavior."

"Care!" she practically yelled. "Who was it that dragged her away from here because they were scared for their precious pigs? I care far more than some in this room, and if I felt she was being destructive, I would let her know. But I find her actions to be perfectly healthy." She smiled as she finished, knowing that this last statement would be particularly irksome to Mr. Porkshire. She hoped that getting under his skin was the fastest way to help him find the door.

"Healthy? You call it healthy to run off with that lazy . . ." Mr. Porkshire was resurrecting all the creative names he had come up with for John when Miss Denine butted in.

"George, as usual you're upset over something you know nothing about. You just rest assured Fannie is with me and is safe. Trust me."

"Trust you? After what you said, I'd sooner trust . . ." Unable to think of someone sufficiently untrustworthy, he was about to settle on "a total stranger," but for dramatic emphasis, he opted rather just to point to a total stranger and say "him!", pointing to a dark corner of the room where a man with a less than impressive stature sat. This was a tactical error, for he had pointed to someone whom he thought was a total stranger, but who was no stranger at all. It was Bishop Goldheart.

Miss Denine had stopped allowing insults of the bishop long ago. Many thought this was because he was her best customer, but as of late, his business had dropped off substantially and her loyalty had not. She did not employ bouncers, having discovered long ago it was more cost effective to offer some able-bodied patron a free beer to toss out the unwanted. Those who frequented her tavern were aware of this practice and were always anxious for someone to throw out. Therefore, as the conversation grew heated between Mr. Porkshire and Miss Denine, almost every man in the tavern moved to the edge of his seat, hoping to get the job of helping Mr. Porkshire and Father Young find the exit.

With an insult of the bishop, Mr. Porkshire had sealed his fate. Miss Denine turned to a table of four stout-looking fellows. Usually, four beers would have been a high price to clear out two men, but she was upset and wanted the job done right. She had not finished saying, "Can you help these gents out?" before all four rose and headed the father's way. He assumed that being a priest and not having partici-pated in the conversation, they would likely handle him more gently. What he failed to take into account was that a free beer was on the line and these men did not want to leave it unclear that they were deserving of it. Two of them grabbed Father Young, hoisted him in the air, and forcefully headed for the door. Before you judge these travelers too harshly, it should be noted that Father Young did hear a faint, "Sorry, Father," just before he was flung through the air. He landed in a large currant bush.

Father Young was not usually inquisitive, but curiosity got the best of him, so as he pulled himself out from the currant bush, he asked the two legs that poked out of the neighboring currant bush, "How do you know Miss Denine?"

Mr. Porkshire wrestled himself into a standing position, removed a few of the more irksome twigs from his trousers and said, "I was in such a rush to get here, I forgot to fill you in. Elizabeth Denine is Mrs. Porkshire's sister. She helped raise Fannie from birth. We lived several miles out of Lushton until we moved to your town. When I first heard she was gone, I assumed she came here—that is, until you said John was also missing. I don't think she'd come here with that . . ." He searched for his favorite words for John, but after rolling them out by the dozens, he found when only one was called for, none came to mind, so he simply said, " . . . that *boy*."

"So, you think she came alone?" Father Young said hopefully.

"I hope so. I would've found out if Elizabeth had been a little more reasonable. Me and Elizabeth have a history, like most family, some good, some bad. But I've come to help me daughter and I'm not leaving till I'm sure she's safe." He said this with a considerable amount of confidence for one who had just been forcefully inserted into a bush.

Father Young worried this confidence might lead them back into the tavern. He had gone his entire life without being thrown out of a bar and didn't wish to make up for lost time. He was relieved when Mr. Porkshire added, "So, we'd better go find John. How did you hire him anyway?"

"Bishop Goldheart sent him."

"Good, where is the bishop?"

Father Young disappointedly pointed at the tavern. "He was the man you pointed at to get us thrown out."

Mr. Porkshire turned as pinkish as any of his prize pets. "Oh . . . well . . . I guess let's try something else."

"You can come out now, Fannie," Miss Denine yelled out as she opened the door to the quarters behind the bar.

"Thanks, Auntie. I wasn't ready to face Father yet."

"Which one?" Miss Denine laughed at her own joke. Fannie also smiled. They walked out to the bar. Miss Denine walked over to a gentleman and after a short conversation looked back to Fannie and said, "Get this man a large beer." She then walked back to Fannie. "And while you do, I think after chasing off your father and a priest I deserve a little bit of an explanation as to why you are here."

Fannie blushed and said, "But before I do, you told my . . . Papa, that you thought what I was doing was perfectly healthy, but you don't really know what I'm doing, at least not yet."

Miss Denine shrugged. "True," she said as she took the beer from Fannie and down to the man who had ordered it. "Clean those mugs." She pointed to a stack in the sink and Fannie began working.

Once the beer had been delivered, she came back to Fannie, and they picked up their conversation as Fannie and Miss Denine began to wash the many mugs collected over the day. "See, Fannie, you came to see me. That is always a good decision, and I trust you. I'm sure whatever reason you had for getting away was a good one."

Fannie smiled. "Thanks."

"So why did you make the trip from Bridgecrest back here?"

"I had to get away. Do you know John the Mason?"

"Oh sure, good looking guy. I thought he was going to marry a girl in town but then he got up and left to fix the church in your town, I think. Word was her parents didn't approve."

"He was going to marry a girl in town? Who?"

"Before I answer that, why do you bring him up? Did he meet someone new in Bridgecrest?" Miss Denine said with a wink.

"Papa told me to avoid him and that I shouldn't be with him. Of course, his ridiculous reason was he thought he didn't like pigs."

With this Miss Denine bent over in a full body laugh. "George and his pigs. It's true," she got out between tears of laughter, "he couldn't respect a man that didn't love pigs."

"Then I told him I hated the pigs and ran off."

Miss Denine tried to stop laughing but the smile continued, "Oh dear, did you run away because you were worried your father wouldn't forgive you for insulting his pigs?"

"Well not exactly. When I ran, I first ran to see John. I told him what my Papa had said, and he said, 'We don't need that fat farmer or anyone else telling us what to do,' and then he told me to run off with him."

Miss Denine's face turned sober, something faces rarely did in her establishment. "What did you say?"

"Nothing, I froze. I eventually got out that it would be good to come back to Lushton again. He said he'd meet me here and then left. I left shortly after. I was just glad I didn't see him on the road. I hardly know what to say to him."

"Well, do you love him?"

"I thought I did, but when he said those things about Papa and told me to run off with him, I began to wonder if I really did. He was just so happy I was mad at my papa because it was clear he didn't want to ask him for my hand. And then he expected me to do what he asked and follow him."

Miss Denine looked directly at Fannie but didn't say anything. Fannie was so glad to be getting this out and, with her aunt looking up into her face, she could see she understood.

"That is what bothered me about Papa. He leaves Lushton without asking me, and then he tells me to drop John without asking me, and then John doesn't even ask if I want to come, he just tells me. Doesn't anyone care about what I want?"

"Freedom," Miss Denine said with a smile. "We all want freedom. Freedom to choose for ourselves. If in the end we have our freedom, need we boast of anything else?"

Fannie turned her head in thought, "Yes, that is it exactly. I want my freedom. I want to be like you. You are truly free. No man tells you what to do. You're not stuck with a pig farmer, listening to him rattle on and on about feed and mud depth. You wanted to start your own place, be your own boss, and you did. That is what I will do. I'll learn from you and stay free from any man telling me what to do."

"Now don't get ahead of yourself. Freedom is a noble goal, but I think you should know a little bit more about both your papa and maybe me before you make too many judgments about who is free."

"What do you mean?"

"Do you know about how your mother and father ended up married?"

"What is there to know? Papa's family were pig farmers since the dawn of time, he probably did what John did and told my mother that she was supposed to marry him, and she did."

"You better have a seat." Miss Denine walked over to the nearby table and pulled up a chair as she said goodbye to the last customer. Fannie took a seat and Miss Denine took a seat facing her. "Your father loved your mother from the moment he laid eyes on her. I remember he was always coming around. Finally, my mum and papa realized it was only a matter of time before he proposed. My family wasn't rich, but we had more than some, and definitely more than your father's family. He is quick to say they were pig farmers but that is only partially true. His father helped tend other men's pigs and livestock, the Porkshires were far too poor to own their own livestock. Sure enough, at some point he came to my parents and asked for your mother's hand. They said no. But he wasn't deterred. He made a deal with the man they were working for that if he did all sorts of extra chores, he would get one of the litters of pigs. For a year your father hardly slept. He worked so hard, and at the end he got his own litter of pigs. Pigs were his ticket to a better life. No one expected him to succeed but he was careful and learned everything he could, and his little herd thrived and grew, and, in a few years, he was doing better than anyone imagined. He went back to my parents and asked again for your mother's hand. By some miracle my parents said yes, but only if he would give them two pigs. In a world where women were supposed to come with a dowry, your father paid two pigs, a very steep price for your mother. And don't think she was an indifferent bystander during all this. They wouldn't have done it even for two pigs if she hadn't spent years begging them. I don't know how many times I had to cover for her because she snuck off to help your father take care of his pigs."

"I guess I can see why they both love pigs so much."

"Now don't get me wrong, all your father's obsession with pigs is far beyond normal. But I can't complain, it was his pig money that helped me pay for this place."

"What?"

"That's right, when I decided to open this place, your father helped me both pay for the materials to build it, and to better show you what kind of people he and your mother are, it was very difficult to pay them back. They kept refusing to take the money I tried to give them. But if you want to be a person who finds what they want and then goes for it, you have some good examples right at home."

Fannie smiled. She had always loved her parents but now she had a newfound respect for them. "Well, what about you, did you always want to run a tavern?"

"Heavens no! I always wanted to marry and settle down, and maybe if the right man ever comes around I still will." Her eyes drifted to an empty table that used to always have her best customer but was more and more as vacant as it was now. "Happiness sometimes isn't about controlling what happens but finding ways to enjoy it. This tavern was the backup plan, but it's been a wonderful one. So, what are you going to do about John?"

"Well, I don't know exactly what I want my future to be, but the more I think about it, I would rather it had pigs in it than John."

Chapter 12

A Heroic Battle

Mr. Porkshire and Father Young realized that being cut off from the communication hub of the city was not going to make success easy. Luckily, it was getting late, and this made the local inn a good option for more than one reason.

Clearly, when Mary and Joseph were looking for a place to stay, they hadn't checked Lushton. There seemed to always be ample room at the inn. Now most hospitality tradesmen in the mid-1500's found it more profitable to combine their inn with a tavern. Lushton's inn did have a tavern, but as noted earlier, most people preferred Miss Denine's for its superior service, superior location, superior food, and when pitting Miss Denine's beauty and kindly demeanor against the bald, portly, angry face displayed by the owner of the inn, everyone agreed the views were far superior as well. Therefore, Mr. Porkshire and Father Young sat alone as they ate their chicken.

"I still can't believe they don't have any pork," Mr. Porkshire complained, staring down at his second-class white meat. Since they had arrived, Mr. Porkshire had been squirming, anxious to move on. If he had had any idea where to find John, he'd have left already.

"Bar keep!" he yelled across the room. "Do you know a golden-haired mason named John?"

The owner, Mr. Durbin, nodded apathetically and went back to cleaning mugs. Father Young couldn't figure out how there were any mugs to clean.

"You wouldn't know where to find him, would you?" Mr. Porkshire continued.

The bar keeper shook his head side to side slightly without looking up. His outgoing nature could have been part of why the place was so busy. He did nothing to cloak the fact that he had no desire to do anything but clean the mugs. So, Mr. Porkshire turned back to his poultry and took a bite. He anxiously twisted the tough meat in his jaw, and before he had completely swallowed, he yelled out, "Do you know anyone who might know?"

This was his third and was soon to be his final question. Mr. Durbin set down the mug and slowly walked to the table. Observing the somberness of the walk and sternness of the face, Father Young was glad they were the only ones there and that there were no travelers that Mr. Dubbin could employ to throw them out. Once at the table, he puffed his chest making himself as large as possible and stated, "Listen, I serve food and beer and keep an inn. If you need gossip, messages, or just someone to talk to, there is another place in town that specializes in that."

Mr. Porkshire was anxious to be leaving anyway, so he took the obvious invitation, dropped a few coins as he stood, and said, "Father, I think I will go out for a bit of air."

Having successfully driven out half of his business for the evening, the bartender turned to Father Young in order to finish the job. Father Young was not prejudiced about which animal was killed for him to enjoy and, therefore, had some desire to finish his meal. But this decision came with the price of enduring Mr. Durbin's gaze, and the longer he stayed, the closer the gaze and the higher the price. Father Young held out for one minute before the pressure got to him and he followed Mr. Porkshire's exit. With the men gone, Mr. Dubbin smiled and finished their meals.

The streets were rather quiet since most of the villagers had retired for the evening. The later the night got, the seedier those patronizing the streets would become. Father Young would usually be in by now, but he felt sufficient time had not passed for him to be prepared to walk past Mr. Durbin's gaze and into his room. He now regretted not walking up to his room to flee that gaze as opposed to going out into the street. Of course, he could have left right when Mr. Porkshire had gone and avoided being alone. The memory of the gaze was still pushing him away when his nerves got the better of him and he started heading back to the inn.

Upon turning down a street near the inn, he noticed a group of young men in the middle of the street playing with a ball. One of the young men poorly kicked it off a building and sent the ball down an alley. Another one of those playing went off after it. Father Young thought he looked familiar and as he came back into view, he realized it was John, the long blond hair was a certain give away. The resemblance caught him off guard because he had never seen him move so quickly before.

The next phase of the Porkshire plan was to find John, but now that he had, Father Young had no idea what to do next. It was good to see that John was not with Fannie. Perhaps they came to Lushton separately? Father Young knew that Mr. Porkshire would confront John, but not feeling that was wise while he was with his friends, decided that discretion was the better part of valor and found a good location behind some crates, squatted, and watched.

Father Young didn't know much about the ball game they were playing, having not been the athletic type, and this made the game awfully boring to watch. Soon, he was struggling to stay awake. Luckily, the men eventually grew tired of chasing the sphere and sat down next to the crates and started to talk.

"Willard, are you ever going to marry Betsy?" one of the men said to another.

"Her father don't think I'm good enough, but once I join the guild they'll think better o' me," he responded.

"What about you, John? We heard you found a fair maid back in Bridgecrest after old Mother Arden threw you out on your ear. Never going to get a shot at another one with a dowry like that."

"This maiden's fairness exceeds riches, and given her father's livestock, a dowry is still on the table," John said with confidence. "Not only that, but a local priest paid me wages just to spend every day with her," he boasted.

Father Young groaned inwardly at this. He lamented ever agreeing to pay John per diem whether or not any work actually got done. His foolishness was John's profit and now doubly so as it became something he could boast to his friends.

"So, what are you doing back in Lushton?" one of them asked. The father leaned in as close as he could without upsetting the crates.

"Just like you, Willard, dear old papa didn't approve."

"So, you gave up?"

"No. I'm sick of letting some girls' parents run my life. I convinced her to come back with me."

The hush of impressed silence fell over the crowded boys. Getting a girl to run off with you against her parents' wishes was not only difficult but quite an edgy approach to life at the time. All the men began to wonder to what extent they had "run off," but no one dared ask.

Through a crack in the carts, Father could see John smiling as his friends clapped him on the back and congratulated him. Something broke loose in Father Young's tortured soul. All those years of watching Fannie from a distance and here John was hinting at her ruined character. As he thought, Father Young's view of John became rather distorted, and John's nose began to enlarge as if Father Young was staring through the bottom of a thick glass at his foe. In the recesses of his mind, he suddenly recalled having a thought in regards to that nose before. It came to him—he had once planned on hitting that nose. The desire came back with more force than before. The original thought had been accompanied by so many caveats. What would happen? How should he do it? What would John do? But this time it came so clear and strong, it was as if a voice from above yelled out, "Smack his nose!" The clarity was now void of any consequences or caveats.

"Did you marry her?" someone finally asked.

"Not yet," John said with pride.

If Father Young's thoughts were a powder keg, then those two words were the spark, and as soon as they left John's mouth, Father Young jumped out, knocked over a few crates, pushed two young men aside, wound up, and hit John on the nose—or, at least, tried. He got a small piece of his nose but mostly cheek and eye. But what he lacked in aim, he made up for in force. John fell to the ground.

What occurred next is difficult to describe in its entirety, as each young man reacted slightly differently. Very few of us are prepared to have a spying priest pop out from a dark street at night and hit our friend in the face, and as these men could attest, the protocol for such situations is not widely understood.

Two men, impressed with the father's strength, decided they did not wish to be the next to test it out, and before even realizing he was a priest, fled the scene. Two others, who looked like they could be brothers, originally turned to fight, but seeing that the father was indeed a priest, figured God had sent him. And although they had never been motivated by any sense of religious piety, they decided that a delayed judgment day would be in their best interest and followed their fleeing companions. Another young man, seeing a priest give John a knocking, felt he must have deserved it, and having witnessed justice served, simply walked away.

So far this was all good news for Father Young, who was busy rubbing his hand and trying not to be too obvious about it. Taking a group of eight down to three in a single blow would be considered quite a victory, or at least it would be if you had any idea what to do with the other three. John still lay on his back, but the two fellows turned to one another, smiled, and then turned to the father. These men were not broad minded, the problem that presented a complication to Father Young's original nose punching plan was that their shoulders did not match their minds. They realized that he was a priest and were not deterred; in fact, they were all the more anxious. These two had been forced to attend church and catechism, and secretly had always hoped for an excuse to "teach" a priest a thing or two. And, in case you think they took it easy on Father Young, you may note that historians would later use this incident as proof that, even in 1550, atheists existed.

What John did doesn't really matter, because before John was able to get up, the other two had started their work. Father Young's first hit was also his last, and his only recollection, after seeing John fall, was these two men headed his way. He didn't know who hit him first but was pretty sure someone did.

The next thing Father Young noticed was water being splashed on his face. And pain. Everything hurt: his head, his body, and his eyes were so swollen he could hardly see. Out of one small slit in his eye, he made out a figure over him. It was Fannie. He smiled, which hurt, and the pain caused him to pass out again.

Father Young woke with a start and immediately pain folded around him. Someone was pouring water on his face. He gave a weak cough and turned his head. Something was wrong with his eyes. He could only make out a tiny sliver of light and a dim figure.

"Lie still," came the angelic voice.

Was that Fannie? He tried to speak, but a fresh wave of pain broke over him and consciousness slipped from him like the men who had disappeared into the night.

Chapter 13

The Passive Patient

Father Young's eyes hesitantly opened as light awoke him. Warmth enveloped him, but he soon realized it was not just from the sunlight. He lay enveloped in a quilt that he soon recognized as not his own. Looking up he found himself in a room full of emptiness. It's only occupants besides the bed he occupied were a single chair and a small table that held a pitcher of water. The pain and swelling were less prominent, but definitely still in attendance. Father Young had no idea what had happened. After seeing the two men walking towards him and blacking out, everything else had been a blur. Had he really heard Fannie's voice? If so, how did she get there and how did he get out of the street? When did he get out of the street? How long had he been asleep? But most of all he wondered how the mission went. Had they gotten to Fannie and John before it was too late? He had to admit, he had added very little to the endeavor. Standing behind Mr. Porkshire while they got thrown out of one place after another probably wasn't of much assistance.

At least he had wounded the enemy prior to his fall, he thought. This brought a smile to his face, and again, severe pain. As the pain continued, a door opened, and in walked Bishop Goldheart. Upon seeing the bishop, he thought of something he hadn't before. Hitting

90

someone in the face was probably a sin and the bishop may be here to address that.

"I'm glad you're awake," Bishop said with a smile. Father Young noticed that the bishop looked younger and more full of energy than he had ever seen him. The bishop's face was bright and he was clearly both happy and sober—something that had evaded him for many years.

Father Young tried to say, "Hello," but trying to open his mouth was too painful and only created a small whimper.

"Relax, Father, don't try to move. Your swelling will go down with time. You really got roughed up. We will have to add a boxing class to the seminary curriculum." The bishop laughed before adding, "I don't want you to worry about getting back to your fold for Mass."

The truth was, Father Young had not thought one second about that, but realized now that perhaps he should have.

"I sent a message to Deacon Morse to take care of your services while we nurse you back to health. And Mr. Porkshire is on his way back to Bridgecrest. He said not to worry about the pigs. He will ensure they are cared for."

Father Young was grateful for all the kindness, but being unable to ask questions, left it up to others to guess what his questions and concerns might be. So far, they were pretty far off the mark.

"Well, I have to get back to the cathedral, but Miss Denine and Fannie have agreed to watch over you."

Father closed his eyes in relief. Fannie was going to be with him! He had worked so long and so hard, traveling to and from her home, listening to lectures on swine, dealing with masons and raising pigs, all to get to know Fannie, and it was finally happening. If only he had socked John in the nose sooner. The pain would all be worth it.

As the bishop walked out, Fannie entered with a curtsy, carrying with her a bowl of soup. "I've brought you some lunch, Father," she said as she sat down on the chair next to the bed. He couldn't think of a time he'd been happier. The soup was wonderful. He sat with half-open eyes and watched Fannie. She sat silently for several minutes before breaking the silence.

"Do you like the soup, Father?"

He slowly nodded.

"I feel so awful. If I'd never left, you wouldn't have been sent off to find John and well you wouldn't be like this."

Father Young wanted to say that it all worked out for the best, but fortunately, he couldn't.

"I hope you get better soon. When I left Bridgecrest, I never thought it might lead to this." Fannie had not intended to make her local priest a confidant, but she felt she had to say something, and without him to respond, her thoughts just began spilling out. "I was so mad. Father told me . . . not you Father, but my other Father, I guess I should say 'Papa' told me to stay away from John. Not that I loved John. Well maybe I thought I did, but deep down I knew Father was right. I just needed space to figure things out on my own—not be told, you know?"

This news brought joy to Father Young greater than his pain and he tried to smile, but that quickly pushed pain back into the lead.

"That was the whole issue. My papa should have trusted me. I'm old enough to figure these things out for myself. I was so mad at Fath . . . I mean Papa, and I needed to get away from it all, both Papa and John."

If there was one thing Father Young understood it was the need to get away from John.

"The one regret I have was the fact that I didn't tell Papa that I was coming to Lushton to think things over, not to run off with John. Aunt Denine has kept John away. Her customers kind of fight over the chance to throw him out the moment he walks in now. I guess no one likes him much. Supposedly, you and Papa just missed him when you came in the other day. Oh, I've been rambling on about things. What you probably want to know is how you got here."

Finally, someone who could guess his questions. He was growing more attached to her by the minute.

"Well, after you and Papa left Aunt Denine's, Papa said he went out looking for John. I'm glad he never found him. He likely would have ended up looking worse than you. Papa found some people who told him where John lives. On the way there, he found you lying in the street. No one is sure exactly what happened to you."

"They thought, at first, that you had been mugged, but your purse was still on you. Papa sent for Bishop Goldheart, and they brought you here to my aunt's place." She got quieter as she said the next part. "Papa said it was because the tavern was closer than the cathedral, but Aunt Elizabeth says Papa knew she wouldn't turn him away with you all bloodied, and he wanted to see me. It worked. You've been sleeping for about a day and a half. Father . . . I mean Papa, wanted to stay until you woke, but someone needed to get back to care for our pigs and yours."

Father Young listened with considerable interest. It was the most he'd ever heard Fannie talk and the more she did, the more he loved her. She was so confident and relaxed around him. People are always apt to show pretense when speaking to others, especially when they don't know them well and even more especially when they are a priest. This made Fannie's calm confidence all that much more a gem to Father Young as she continued. When one is unable to speak, they have a lot of time to think, and for Father Young, that led to a lot of exalted thoughts about Fannie. Before long he could have given you several pages of positive adjectives that would only begin to define Fannie. And perhaps of all the compliments he would add that even the subject of pigs didn't irritate him when it flowed from her lips.

For the next week, Father Young made significant progress on his original quest to get to know Fannie. In fact, he knew Fannie better than anyone alive. While he continued to improve, cuts and bruises around his face still made talking painful, but he enjoyed listening to Fannie so much that he didn't mind not speaking. It became rather a pattern in their relationship.

Father Young became a sort of benign, living diary where she could vent her thoughts without any chance of criticism or interruption. She was comfortable saying whatever she wanted, and he was comfortable simply listening, watching, and enjoying.

He was pleasantly surprised with how well-educated Fannie was. Her parents and Miss Denine had filled her full of all sorts of useful information. She knew many home cures and remedies and tried various herbal concoctions on his bruises and cuts. Some were effective, and some left much to be desired. But the father was a model patient and even sat still when boiled stinging nettle was applied.

But even better than her remedies were her abilities as a storyteller. She knew tales of the Norman conquest and of King Arthur and his knights. She also knew many of the stories of the Bible and Father Young loved her retailing of the plagues of Egypt and of the Savior's birth. When telling of Samson, she jumped from her chair and grabbed a large spoon for a jawbone yelling, "Take that ye dirty Philistines!" She swung and thrust and jumped before turning to the father and saying, "I won't actually reenact killing all one thousand, I imagine that took Samson a bit of time." And even under his bruises you could see blushing as she batted her eyes and looking directly at Father said, "Oh Samson, if you really loved me, you would tell me how you get to be so very strong? Don't you love me?"

Father Young used to think Samson a fool for telling Delilah it was his hair that gave him his strength. As he sat looking at Fannie, he decided he would not judge Samson so harshly in the future.

Father Young could see that Fannie loved learning and adventure. He thought of the books in his library that she would love to read. This thought reminded him that reading was not something Fannie could do, but he could tell she would love it. The thought of cold nights by a fire with her in his arms as he taught her the thing that so few women had access to at the time. The world would be opened to her. He began to imagine the adventures that he could give to her not only in books but in life, if they could only be together.

So, while Father Young got to know Fannie, Fannie still knew precious little about the father, which is why it may surprise some to learn that, over the course of the week, Fannie fell very much in love with Father Young. Despite what she did not know about Father Young, he did come off as a very good listener, better than any man she had ever been acquainted with. He listened, smiled, and, even though it pained him, he laughed from time to time. In fact, men would do well to learn from Father Young. When Zacharias was struck dumb by the angel for disbelieving his aged wife could conceive a child, it may have been less about punishing his lack of faith, and more about endearing his wife to him enough to make the miracle possible.

The other ironic advantage the father had over other men was weakness. While most men would strive to impress a girl with machismo, hoping to tap into her desire for protection, the father showed up on the very opposite end of that spectrum: a beaten, helpless man, and unwittingly tapped into a more powerful female instinct, that of mothering. Caring for someone so weak and helpless who had no other source of healing brought that mothering instinct into full force for Fannie. This not only provided the father with the tireless service and kindness that stands as the scientific wonder of motherhood, but also induced the kind of compassion usually reserved for tiny infants in their own helpless state. What man can compete with an infant for a woman's affections? Many unfortunate woodsmen have learned the answer to this question when they have unwittingly stumbled between a she bear and her cub. Fannie was now experiencing this power, but somehow Father Young became both an infant and the humblest of silent men, and the combination was irresistible.

A word of caution, however, to those men who might be taking notes. The former quality of excellent listening and near silent but enrapt attention to your lady can be emulated, as much as one's ego will permit, with very favorable results. However, the latter strategy of drawing out the mothering instinct by appearing completely weak and helpless cannot be recommended universally to those wishing to engender affection rather than disgusted resentment from their beloved. Unfortunately, the sudden inability to do anything for oneself must originate from actual catastrophic events which would put a man in too close of contact with death to be an advisable strategy. It was simply an act of serendipity, along with blunt force, that rendered Father Young thus incapacitated and recipient of this unique affection.

Communication is often a struggle for lovers. With how poorly some communicate it is a wonder they don't end up killing themselves over it. Now wouldn't that be a story, but I digress. Father Young and Fannie were no exception. Besides the obvious issue that half of the participants were unable to speak, Fannie was being open on every issue except for her love of Father Young. And who can blame her? What good would it do? Fannie may have been progressive, but the idea of her professing her love to a man was unthinkable, even if she did think about it. Then, there was the pesky, sworn life of celibacy to consider. She couldn't see any way around that one that didn't involve heresy, excommunication, joblessness, or a very long platonic courtship that could only end in death or her marriage to someone else.

So, Father Young lay ignorant of her love. She seemed friendly and, indeed, she *was* friendly. She seemed to be enjoying herself, but she always seemed to enjoy herself. It was one of the many things he loved about her. Plus, as far as he knew, she was *assigned* to care for him. While men are apt to confuse females who are simply good employees with being in love with them, the father was cautious to assume too much and, therefore, figured she was simply a good employee or kind soul.

So, while both lovers grew more in love, they remained ignorant of the other's feelings. Ignorance didn't bother either party. It rarely does. They were happy just enjoying each other's presence. But like all things in life, their happiness was not without a price. Their enjoying the company of the other meant that those who usually had their company were without it.

In the case of Father Young, that price was small. While many in his congregation enjoyed his ability as a priest, they could go a few weeks without him. In fact, many of his parishioners had taken his absence as a good excuse to miss Mass and were anxious that he take all the time he needed to fully recover. He knew that those who were really missing him were limited to Mr. Porkshire and his pigs. He was convinced Mr. Porkshire would survive, and he hoped the pigs wouldn't.

However, Fannie was another story. Everyone enjoyed her company. Her aunt loved having her in Lushton but was growing weary of giving out free beers to have John thrown out. The person most distressed by Fannie's absence was Mrs. Porkshire. Upon arriving home, Mr. Porkshire had told her where Fannie was. He assured her she was okay, but that only calmed her for a time. She missed her only daughter. This absence may have made the heart grow fonder but did not make the heart grow stronger. Mrs. Porkshire had become ill, or at least, very depressed. The two can be difficult to distinguish between.

It had progressed enough that even Mr. Porkshire was worried. Despite being reluctant to call her back, he decided it was time for Fannie to come home. It was with sorrow that Fannie received the news from Peter the messenger. She worried about her mother but hated to leave Father Young. She was reluctant to leave without saying goodbye, but the father was currently asleep. She needed time, but Peter had been hired to play messenger and escort. This would ensure that no masons attempted to take the latter job. Miss Denine insisted she leave now since Father Young was not likely to wake for hours. Very reluctantly, she agreed. But as they walked down the hall to the exit, Fannie suddenly said, "I've left my gloves in Father Young's room. Let me get them, and we can go."

Miss Denine was confused. She didn't think Fannie had gloves.

There he lay, still very bruised, but a hundred times dearer to her than when they'd first met. The past week had flown by. It felt like yesterday that she had been running from John. At that time, Father Young was a footnote in her life. Now, she couldn't comprehend life without him. She wanted desperately to stay, to be by his side as he healed, as he spoke again, walked again, and essentially came back to life before her eyes. She stood just looking at him. She put a hand forward and touched his cheek. He smiled, still sleeping—a reflex to her soft touch that now entered his dreams. She leaned forward. Just then she heard steps coming. She was taking longer than expected. No doubt, Miss Denine was coming to check on her.

In the rush of emotion, as footsteps headed her way, her judgment gave way to desire. She brushed her lips against his cheek then headed for the door. "Coming! I guess I didn't leave them here."

Lost in sleep and dreams, the smile on the father's face grew wider.

Chapter 14

A Damsel in Distress

When he awoke, Father Young heard the slight noises of someone by the bedside. A smile had begun to form on his face as he turned, expecting to see Fannie. It was Miss Denine. His head shot back, and his eyes grew large.

"I know I don't look as good as I once did, but I didn't think I looked that bad. And I don't like to be cruel but, Father, you are in no condition to critique people's looks."

Father Young did his best to smile. While Fannie's presence had helped his recovery, her absence was able to work miracles. In that moment, he found the strength to sit up and say the first words he'd spoken in over a week.

"Where's Fannie?" he croaked, his voice rusty from lack of use.

Miss Denine didn't know changing nurses would induce such a shock. She calmed Father Young and got him to lie back down. She was unaware of what she was dealing with. She thought she was handling someone who had been within an inch of his life. She had no idea the real issue was something as serious as love. If she had only known, she would not have been so casual.

"She had to go back to be with her folks. She left yesterday."

Father Young hadn't even tried talking during the last few days. Now he found it wasn't as painful as he thought—not comfortable, but not excruciating. His emotions overcame the discomfort. "She didn't come to say goodbye?" he questioned.

"You were asleep. Now calm down and eat your soup."

Well, that was it, thought Father Young. *Fannie had only been here out of kindness or at her aunt's request and had now happily skipped on to her next assignment.* The small notion that Fannie cared for him was blown out like a candle in a hurricane.

With his new caregiver, his health improved rapidly. His paradise had turned into a prison and his recovery was accelerated by his desire to get out. It wasn't that Miss Denine wasn't an accommodating host. She was. But she was also busy. He rarely saw her and, being alone, confined to a bed, led to very boring days. Father Young attempted to walk the day he found out Fannie left, even though he probably wasn't ready for it. He was determined to free himself from the shackles of nothingness. Some have said laughter is the best medicine, but Father Young now discovered the amazing medical benefits of boredom.

Within a day, he had done enough laps around the room that he was prepared to go out and walk. Anything besides these grey, wood-planked walls would be a beautiful sight to behold. So, with that in mind, he headed out the door.

Once out the door, Father Young found he was in a hallway. Down to his right, he could hear the clamor of the tavern. He decided to head that way. For one thing, he didn't know where the other direction led, and at the bar, he knew he would likely find Bishop Goldheart. He hadn't spoken with the bishop since he first awoke, and the bishop might be able to shed more light on exactly what had happened to him that night. Upon opening the door to the bar, Miss Denine quickly turned to him, not accustomed to people entering from the back rooms.

"Oh, Father. It's so good to see you up and about. Come out for a bit to eat?" she kindly asked.

"No." Talking was still uncomfortable and he did his best to balance brevity with manners. "Bishop?"

The title which Father Young was sure would lead to Miss Denine pointing to a table where he sat, had no such effect. Rather, a dark scowl came over Miss Denine's face. "Oh, Bishop Goldheart? Don't ask me where he is. Why would he be here anyways? He must be too busy for our company." She quickly scuttled off, clearly irritated by the subject. Father Young couldn't have been more surprised.

Still anxious to get out, he decided he would give the bishop a visit. As he exited, he noticed himself in the looking glass that sat on the far wall. He looked awful. Eyes still blackened, nose swollen, and with a slightly misaligned jaw, he looked more like some sort of monster than a priest. He realized women and children might flee at the sight of him. Frightening children had never been a goal of his, but he did want to get out, so off he went.

Within a hundred yards of the tavern, Father Young had his first chance to determine how people would react to his face as a mother and grown daughter were walking towards the tavern. Father Young almost wanted to walk head held high and get their true reaction but as he approached his courage faltered. He turned his head away and down as he approached them and listened for the sounds of them scuffling past him. Instead, footsteps slowed and stopped. "Father, it is so good to see you on this beautiful day."

He looked up fearing the worst. As his scars and altered face came into view, the father saw in amazement that the smile on her face only grew. This woman was beaming as much as he'd ever seen someone beam. "It is a lovely day," the father got out.

"Father, I always count it a blessing to see a man, as yourself, dedicated to God. I cannot help but think that you see more in the world than the rest of us."

Father Young's voice was not in a condition to be giving sermons on what he saw in the world and wasn't sure he would be up to it if he could. Not only that, he wasn't so sure he saw "more" in the world than anyone else. He allowed his head to bounce somewhere between a nod and shake, sort of a semicircular motion.

She continued, "I, a humble woman, who needs to learn so much in my godly walk, ask that you accept this gift as a way for me to show my respect for the life that you choose to live." She held out an apple as she bowed. Father was shocked. Apples, while the most common fruit, were still a luxury and it was rare for a peasant to get one, let alone give it away.

"I couldn't," Father Young got out.

"I insist." She continued to hold out the apple, and Father Young paused but finally took it.

"Much thanks," he said and bowed.

"Oh, you are a great man," she said as she rose, bringing a hand to her chest. "Father, would you permit me to introduce you to my dear daughter?" She motioned to her daughter who had stood silently by her mother during this interchange. The daughter now stepped forward and both mother and daughter looked up at the father, waiting for a response.

Father Young did not feel it was his place to deny anyone the ability to introduce someone else, so he simply nodded.

"This is Katherine, she is the best of my children, obedient and kind. She is handy with a needle and the clothes she wears are of her own making. She is a hard worker and would be a good benefit to anyone with a garden or in raising animals. Is she not beautiful?"

Father Young again was perplexed by the question. Not that he couldn't see her beauty but why was he the one to judge? And why was this mother giving him her daughter's resume? He again nodded but added as quickly as possible. "Thank you. But I must be going." And resumed his walk past this kind family.

He wasn't sure how long this mother had planned to continue her discussion on the positive attributes of her daughter, but he could sense she would have let it go on if he had. As he walked off, he could hear her stammering out an excuse to get him to stay. He ignored the stammering and continued his walk towards the cathedral.

Within a short distance, another woman and daughter approached. Father Young could be mistaken but it looked like they were headed towards him. Before they got too close, he decided to take a short turn and sure enough, as he did the mother began to hasten her pace and follow down the path towards Father Young. "Oh Father, it is such a blessing to see a man of God out on this beautiful day. How wise of you to choose this path. Is it not God who has put us together?"

What was with these questions? The only thing he liked about them is that he could answer them with a nod.

"I feel that as a gift for the example you lead it is only appropriate for me to bestow this bread to you." She held out a loaf of bread as she too bowed.

"I really couldn't."

"Oh, it would bring me such joy to share what God has given me after you give so much to God."

Father Young reluctantly took the bread.

"Father, I would like you to meet my daughter, Ruth, she is the healthiest of my children. She is an expert in caring for children, having helped me raise six. She never tires or talks back, and indeed, God has blessed her so that she will be able to birth many children."

"Thank you, I must be going," Father Young said as he headed back to the main path. The whole situation was uncomfortable, but he did not need to worry about the women in Lushton's ability to birth future generations.

As he walked, Father Young puzzled about these women's sudden impulses to introduce him to their daughters. Mothers were proud of their daughters. He knew this. But they'd always been proud of them. Why today was the official talk-about-your-daughter day, he could not guess. But he had little time to ponder this because it happened again. And again. He was now walking with an apple, a loaf of bread, a small shawl, and a goat on a leash.

He was walking rather quickly away from his most recent mother and daughter encounter when, out of a patch of trees, a young maiden screamed and fell toward the ground in front of Father Young. He lurched forward to stop her fall, but he wasn't experienced in woman catching, and she, an apple, and a loaf of bread all fell through his arms and into the mud. The goat was running off behind him as he quickly helped her up. He looked up and down the road. How she had fallen or where she had come from was a mystery. She must have entered very suddenly or the onslaught of young ladies in a few short blocks had dulled his senses' ability to notice them.

Now upright, she rattled off, "Oh, Father, thank you for catching . . . I mean trying to catch me."

Looking at her, Father Young now suspected why she had fallen. She was rather top heavy. Just then, another woman came out of the trees. "Father, I see you have met my daughter Mary."

Father Young nodded kindly and started to walk away before the forest could produce any more random women. Mary's mother pushed her forward and they joined in step and began to follow, but before long Father Young heard, "Welcome to our town, Father. May I introduce you to my daughter Esther?" Father Young turned and saw a woman with a girl that appeared around the age of ten.

"She can help you find where you are going," the mother insisted, pushing the girl forward.

"No need," Mary's mother said as she pushed Mary right next to Father Young.

"I will guide him," Mary said, taking his arm as her mother gave the other woman and daughter a glare.

Father Young had never had a female this close to him. Despite Mary's over-aggression, he had to admit it felt nice to have her hold his arm.

"So where are we going, Father?" she asked with a smile, as he heard a collective groan from the quorum of women behind him.

"Bishop," is all he got out, not knowing whether it was pain or nervousness that restricted his voice more.

Father Young did not know if he should be seen arm in arm with a female in the streets, from time to time he would pull away slightly and Mary would simply pull him in tighter.

The flow of women continued to find Father Young. But now they only approached, saw Mary, scowled, and then stomped off.

Once at the cathedral, Father wondered if a festival was about to start. The streets next to the cathedral were twice as busy as he'd ever seen. It was as if all Lushton had moved shop and planted themselves outside the cathedral. Street vendors sold goods; groups of people conversed. Upon closer inspection, Father Young noticed they all had something in common. The cathedral was surrounded by women.

Once at the door, Mary smiled and patted his arm, "Well, here we are. I'll see you soon."

Father Young entered and went straight back to the bishop's attached living quarters. Father Young knocked and heard the bishop slightly crack the door. "Oh, it's just you, Father Young. I thought it was Mrs. Jedds bringing her daughter and more cookies." Bishop

Goldheart motioned Father Young to come in quickly and shut and bolted the door behind them.

Father Young didn't have to ask. The bishop knew he had pain speaking and could read the question on his face. "You want to know why mothers and daughters are mobbing this place? They probably mobbed you on your way in."

Father Young nodded.

The bishop leaned in and spoke softly, "It's Father Smith from Dellshire. He got married. Word has spread and people have learned about Article 32. While the articles are not yet law, it's clear that we're allowed to marry, or at least no one will stop us. Suddenly we are eligible bachelors, and no one finds this more exciting than the mothers of single daughters."

Father Young's mind reeled. He hadn't foreseen this problem. Being able to marry, in his mind, only meant he could be free to court Fannie. He hadn't thought it would make all the women free to court *him*.

Father Young's difficulty in speaking left it incumbent on the bishop to carry the conversation. "So, Father Young, once we get you all healed up, you'll be free to go marry your Fannie."

Father Young wished he saw it as simply as the bishop did. He had tried with his might over the past year to get to know her and had yet to have a two-way conversation with the girl.

While his situation and the recent changes in church policy had improved his chances with Fannie, he knew his ability to interact with the opposite sex had not. Plus, he knew that during the time that Fannie had spent with him he had hardly looked his best.

While the bishop saw Father Young's case as open and shut, he saw all too clearly the intricacies and stumbling blocks of his own situation. He had never opened up to anyone about Miss Denine. It was his burden to carry. Plus, being a bishop, it was his job to carry others' burdens, not encumber them with his own. He looked up to the father and realized if there was anyone who might understand it was the man sitting in front of him.

"Father Young, I understand your love for Fannie. I too . . . well love is not foreign to me." Father Young's eyes showed that he didn't understand. "I guess what I am trying to say is I too have loved, or love." There was another long pause. He looked to the father for a response, but the father didn't know what to say and as the two sat in awkward silence, the bishop finally said, "It is Miss Denine. She has my heart, my mind, my soul. I love her deeply." With this he stood and turning his back to Father Young, he looked out the window.

Father Young could not have been more stunned. Wrapped up in his own problems, he had assumed he was the only priest who had experienced love. Oh, he knew of priests who had succumbed to that evil, the evil of lust, but he did not assume a fellow of the cloth had as true a love as his, especially not his own bishop. He suddenly realized, maybe true love's course was smooth for no one.

"I have loved her for years," continued the bishop as he looked out over the back of the cathedral. "Everything about her, her hair, her eyes . . ." The bishop's eyes grew glassy as he dreamily continued, "Her cheeks, the way she walks, the way she turns when having cleared a table . . ."

Father Young tapped his foot on the floor, bringing the bishop out of his daydream.

"Oh. Um. Well, you see what an awful mess this whole Article 32 thing is, don't you?"

In no way did Father Young see what a mess it was. To Father Young, the bishop's case seemed as open and shut as Father Young's did to the bishop. His continued silence on the subject allowed the bishop to explain.

"For years, I have been a faithful customer of Miss Denine's. It gave me a chance to see her, to be with her. There was no expectation that I would do anything. No one expected a bishop of wanting—I mean, of loving someone in that way. Now she'll know. She'll figure it out. She'll know that I must be there because of my love for her. And how could she possibly welcome the affection of a man like me?"

Father Young thought that constantly ordering drinks and getting drunk might provide the bishop a viable explanation for being at a bar but didn't interrupt.

"Not only that, but what am I supposed to do? I have never courted, never wooed, nor sought after a wife. No. I am too scared. I can't go back. Oh, how I long to see her again, but it cannot be."

Having admitted it, Bishop Goldheart seemed somewhat less agitated, and this allowed him to turn his mind to his guest.

"This Article 32 has been complicated for me, but it is wonderful for you. Just think, you will be the first priest I will marry. Oh, it will be a lovely service . . ."

As the bishop went on about spring blossoms and bluebirds, Father Young's mind drifted to the fact that he and the bishop were much in the same predicament. Being raised and tutored as men of the cloth, they found their ability to interact with the opposite sex completely lacking. Father Young couldn't help but feel that if he helped the bishop and Miss Denine find happiness, it might lead to his own wedded bliss.

So now he had a mission. After all, he couldn't do much wooing back in Bridgecrest, that is, until he got his face and voice back. Now it was time for him to play matchmaker.

Chapter 15

The Matchmaker

With a goal now set in his mind, it was time to exit. Father Young nodded to say, "Thanks for your time, bishop, but I must be on my way," but that is hard to convey in a nod. So, Bishop Goldheart assumed the father was responding to his question as to whether he wanted the wedding to be in Bridgecrest.

After the nod, the bishop said, "Of course, Bridgecrest, it must be there. Why would it be anywhere else?"

So, the bishop went on and on about that, and a half hour later, Father Young was finally being ushered to the exit.

With the exit in sight, he now had his next goal in mind. The tavern was his next target. Somehow, he had to get Miss Denine and the bishop in the same room. Little did he realize he was not to be a runner headed for the finish line as much as the baton. Waiting at the door to receive him from Bishop Goldheart was Mary.

Back into Mary's arms the father went. Like a baby being handed to an overbearing aunt, no matter how he disagreed with what was occurring, he was helpless to prevent it.

Giving the bishop a look that begged sanctuary back at the church did no good. He had already turned away, and no look, no matter how pathetic, would turn him around.

"So, Father, where are we off to?" Mary asked, grinning from ear to ear. "First, mustn't we go around north to get Mother again?" The distinct lack of the word "my" in the sentence bothered Father Young. No part of "mother" did he want ownership of. Not only that, but Mary was also a force he could scarcely reckon with. He certainly knew he was helpless when both her and her creator were to be reckoned with. So, as violently as he was able, he shook his head back and forth, continuing long after she recognized it to ensure there was no misinterpretation.

Mary huffed and looked to the side. It was time for option two. The biggest issue with option two was its lack of existence. Mary's specialty in life was smiling and tripping over things, not long-term planning. Thinking and walking were causing a strain on her poor cerebrum, not accustomed to so much activity. Her brain was able to communicate down the spine to the leg to move. And her leg was not disobedient but confused. The brain, in its effort to communicate with the leg and come up with a new location to escort the priest, had neglected to tell the leg in which direction to move.

The leg wanted to obey, but the command "move" had never been singular before. So, the leg paused, continued, and ultimately made a triumphant push forward. The left leg was beaming with pride, having been put in a nearly impossible situation and rising to it, it now waited for the next order. All would have remained well if the brain had only realized which direction the left leg had chosen, it would not have directed the right leg to cross through it. Soon the mind had to abandon both giving directions to the legs and option two and instead focus on survival. Every arsenal in the poorly equipped brain was used to stop the brain's sudden downward motion.

Beyond the shortcomings of Mary's upper chambers were two fortunate circumstances beyond her power. For no matter Father Young's personal feelings about Mary, he could not let a damsel fall without making a valiant effort at preserving life. The other was a peddler, peddling flowers.

In your mind, you may see the flower peddler. Every person has to deal with prejudices, but none like the flower peddler of Lushton. For what all flower peddlers were meant to be, he was not. For one, he was a he. The other regular criteria: dainty, calm, flowery, kind, smiley, warm, and personable, he was not. Rough, gruff, coarse, rude, large, cold, and rugged he was. But perhaps it was good he was this way because making it as a flower girl wasn't easy in the Dark Ages.

Therefore, the reason the gruff peddler's presence was good for Mary had nothing to do with him, but rather, the fact that his goods were just as soft as he was hard. As her flailing arms tried to lessen the fall, they simply warded off Father Young's attempts at saving her and she rolled out of the father's arms into a pile of flowers.

The smell of the roses and the swirl of pink, orange, red, blue, and lavender petals instantly took one hundred percent of Mary's attention and she forgot she had fallen. All she knew was she was bathed in petals. Looking up, she saw Father Young standing over her. Her dreams were coming true. Bathing in flowers with a wealthy suitor looking over her was her destiny, and it had arrived. She grabbed an armful of flowers where her favorite color was most abundant and accepted Father Young's helpful hand.

Mary arose from the flowery cushion, and with quite different expressions, there the three stood. Mary smiled and peered at both men. Father Young, shocked, first turned to look at Mary, perplexed by her instant happiness, then looked at the peddler. The peddler, knowing Mary was too clueless to realize the damage she had caused and recognizing her inability to pay for it, turned his focus, with a grinning stare, solely on Father Young.

As they shared glances, Father Young's eyes questioned, "What do you want me to do?"

The peddler stared back, his body language easy to read. "Someone's paying for this."

Both men turned to Mary, who said out of her grinning mouth, "I love flowers." Then she took a deep sniff of those she still grasped in her arms.

The peddler's eyes turned from Father Young's face to his coin purse. Father Young had no desire to purchase flowers but one look at the huge arms crossed over the flower man's chest and he knew it was time to pay. As enjoyable as his first recovery had been, he decided it was best not to begin round two.

Mary saw Father Young's purse as he pulled it out and paid the man for the flowers. The peddler conveniently charged double his usual price, realizing the father had little choice in the matter. As the coins traveled from Father Young's purse to his hand and then into the palms of the peddler, Mary's mind computed what was going on. Father Young was buying her flowers. While this was true, it left out some important details. But to Mary, not only was this the convenient part of the story to hold onto, but it was also the only part of the story witnessed by the group of peasants that now came around the corner.

Leading that group was our dear friend Henry from Bridgecrest. See, Henry, like everyone else, was all a buzz about Article 32. However, unlike most people who had a priest in their town, Henry had the unfortunate situation of having his priest out-of-town when it was announced. Therefore, Henry quickly found out Father Young's whereabouts and headed to Lushton. Secretly, he had hoped Father Young had run off to Lushton to court a secret love whom he had kept hidden for years. Now, as his eyes caught hold of Father Young purchasing flowers for a woman, his heart raced, he knew it was all true. Being among the first to see the proof of Father Young's devotions, felt to a gossip connoisseur like himself as if he had just witnessed his first miracle toward sainthood. He now found himself torn between gathering more evidence and sharing what little he had already collected. Decision came quickly as he couldn't think of any action more definitive than purchasing flowers, plus, he could always add a few embellishments. If a warm embrace did not occur right then, it surely already did or soon would occur. So off he went to spread the news of Father Young's attachment.

Except for a few minor stumbles by Mary, the rest of the walk was uneventful. Among the excitement of falling and receiving gifts from Father Young, her poor, overstimulated brain had forgotten all about plan B. Therefore, Father Young's footsteps played guide and before long, they were back at the tavern.

Even with Father Young heading directly to the tavern, they did not travel as fast as Henry's news. Most of Lushton quickly knew that Mary and Father Young had long loved each other and now that priests could wed, had taken their love from closed doors and secret notes to the openness of the public streets.

This news left a good portion of the population in dismay. Enterprising women and mothers couldn't believe the good fortune of living in Lushton where, when Article 32 was discovered, they had two men of the cloth in residence, thus doubling their prospects. To have their hopes cut in half so soon was disheartening. Perhaps it was the dislike of disheartedness that led several to ask for something not usually required of gossip, namely proof.

The proof was in the flowers. All of Lushton knew Mary's forwardness almost rivaled her ability as a klutz but why, if it were one-sided, would Father Young travel here from Bridgecrest and buy her flowers? With the eye-witness tale of a romantic purchase, no one dared dispute the facts. It was with glee that Henry related the tale to a large group huddled around him at the tavern. "I doubt you'll be seeing much of Father Young without Mary in tow." The front door swung open and there they appeared, arm in arm.

The verdict was in. Father Young was Mary's and Mary was his. While this might limit the pursuits of other women, it would only encourage Mary, for none would love such rumors more than she.

Father Young had wanted to play matchmaker, but he couldn't even leave his room without Mary snatching him up. While he had no proof, he was confident she had been sleeping outside his door.

He found it impossible to avoid her. All his mental powers were being used on complex schemes to get rid of her and that left no time to scheme how to get the bishop and Miss Denine together. He even thought of abandoning his quest at matchmaking and returning to Bridgecrest to get rid of Mary. He had even said on one of the walks where Mary appeared out of nowhere to suddenly be on his arm, "Mary, I will have to be getting back to Bridgecrest soon."

She kindly smiled and said, "Oh I can't wait to see Bridgecrest! I hear it's beautiful." And that ended that plan.

The only thing he had accomplished in the past two days was faster reflexes. He had gotten quite adept at catching the falling Mary. Practice does make perfect. With each trip, stumble, or fall, somehow, he almost instantly made a full body catch. She would always look up with dreamy eyes, giggle, and say, "Oh, Father."

Inevitably, someone would at that instant turn a corner to see them in this embarrassing posture. Rumors of people catching Father Young and Mary in warm embraces with the former about to endow a wet kiss on the latter were becoming so commonplace that it was difficult to find someone willing to listen to the whole tale.

This bothered no one more than Henry. He was so anxious to tell his story again and again that he found it rather annoying to have had such inside information suddenly no longer very informative. In time, he determined that it was time to head back to Bridgecrest where his stories would be appreciated. However, before he left, he decided to tell one more person, with the hopes of making the big time. With this in mind, he stopped by the inn, got the best parchment he could find, and began writing.

Perhaps the one accomplishment Father Young had acquired beyond improved reflexes, were vastly improved vocal cords. They were better than they had ever been, on account of getting plenty of rest. He had nothing to say to her. Mary had plenty to say, but her thoughts had to be sent from her mind to her mouth, so they never quite reached their destination. Therefore, most of their walks were spent in silence. As far as other people, they all seemed to avoid their company except for the few moments when they turned corners into them. His mental efforts were mostly spent on plotting his escape, avoiding eye contact, and wondering what moral men did in such predicaments. As their walks went on, he began to see more than ever the joys of a celibate life. Being without love he had always seen love as a rather simple game. Meet, fall in love, and live a simple existence happily with your love by your side.

Does anyone get to marry who they love? he pondered. Perhaps men are all doomed to marry a Mary, the first woman who thrust themselves upon them. For what could a man do? No gentleman, knight, scholar, or other name that people use for the upper tier of manhood, could call himself thus if he went about telling perfectly kind young ladies that he would rather embrace celibacy than continue to endure their company. Or at least, not anymore. Good Queen Elizabeth had put an end to a man's only legitimate excuse for bachelorhood.

Even as he began to long for his old celibate excuse, deep down he had not forgotten his Fannie. He knew even if celibacy were still on the table, it would not make him happy. At one point, he thought of telling Mary he had grown fond of celibacy and couldn't give it up, and then marry Fannie anyhow. But two things stopped him. One was the inevitable fact that Mary would find out, and the other, that one pesky commandment, that thou shalt not bear false witness. It weighed heavy on his mind of late. In fact, almost all his schemes to rid himself of Mary seemed to fall apart because of that one commandment. In the future, he would show more mercy when people came to confession for that one.

No matter how he saw things, it looked rather bleak, and he found himself attempting a constant balance to try to ignore her while being prepared to save her from sudden downward motion at any second.

It was these bleak and dark projections of his future that led to his lethargy on the third morning since the flower incident. He had no desire to rise. He knew it would only bring further walks with Mary. As he was deciding the possibility of getting up and wondering if there was any other option, there came a knock at his door. Mary was moving the playing field, he thought. All he could think to say was, "Come in," and he had no desire to say it, so silence won out.

"Father, may I come in?" came Miss Denine's voice through the door as she cracked it open.

Miss Denine had continued her gracious ways even as Father Young appeared to be more healed and less in need. "I noticed you weren't up, and I wondered if you wanted some breakfast."

Hunger was not pressing him, but he was grateful to have the meal brought to him where he could dine alone, something he hadn't done for some time.

"You know, Father, Mary was first in the tavern this morning. I'm sure she'd love to eat with you," Miss Denine said.

Father Young was not accustomed to speaking freely, and he simply said, "In here is fine."

"My business would fail if I couldn't successfully read people," Miss Denine said, "and your face is telling it all. If you don't like Miss Mary, I wouldn't recommend spending so much time with her."

Father Young was not opposed to advice, but he didn't find much value in the advice just offered. So, he asked, "Miss Denine, how shall

I accomplish this task of not spending much time with her?" He was not expecting a good answer.

This was a difficult conversation for him to have. As a priest, he was not accustomed to opening up with your run-of-the-mill peasant, especially a female and especially, in matters of the heart. Yet desperation and frustration overruled judgment as he continued. "I have tried to not spend time with her. She's always there. I even tried the back door. She must have had a lookout because within five steps, she was linked arm in arm with me."

"I was unaware of your plight, Father. I am sorry to say that I let the rumors outweigh my better judgment and believed you had fallen for her as hard as she so often does in my tavern. If I only knew." She was quickly lost in thought. But before long she continued. "I believe we can get you out without Mary's knowledge. Where would you like to go?"

It was the hope of being without Mary that allowed his mind to more freely operate, and he now recalled his task of three days before. "Can you get me to see the bishop?"

Father Young could see that was not the choice Miss Denine would have made, but her goodness got the better of her. "All right. I'll smuggle you out of here in one of the large kegs and take you to the cathedral."

Father would have preferred plan B. He didn't know what plan B was, but he was sure he would prefer it. However, Miss Denine spoke with such decisiveness, there was no room for objection.

Within a few minutes, Miss Denine had rolled a large keg into Father Young's room. One would call this a large keg when comparing it to other kegs. However, thinking of it as a dwelling for personal accommodation made one rethink the term "large." It was with considerable exertion, pain, and some noises he never thought he'd make, that he finally crammed himself into it. Miss Denine rested the lid atop, which did not quite close. That is, it didn't close until she gave it a few quick, heavy blows with her surprisingly strong fist.

Then the rolling began. Father Young wished Miss Denine had chosen a new keg or at least had put a more valiant effort into cleaning this particular one out. The constant rolling end over end he felt he could handle but combined with the smell of the year-old remnant of ale and his breakfast was on the rise.

Straining his mind, he tried to remember why it was he was hiding in this keg about to vomit. Had being accosted by Mary really been that bad? But he didn't allow himself to think too long on the subject. He was where he was and needed to focus his energy on keeping his stomach in place. After all, half-digested breakfast would not improve the smell.

Back at the tavern, Mary was getting anxious. Father Young had never taken so long to arise. She checked the door over and over. The sound of the rolling keg had made her jump, and she assumed it must be Father Young coming down the hallway. However, only Miss Denine and a keg went by. She sat back down, but what if something had happened to him? Not much longer and she was determined she'd head to the back and enter his room if need be.

The roadway was not well graded, and each bump or rock was transferred directly to Father Young's sides. Luckily, the keg was not well secured on the wagon so it rolled back and forth. Therefore, as jabs entered, different parts of his side were affected, keeping the pain evenly spread.

Somehow between jabs and smells and focusing on his stomach, Father had time to contemplate what to do. While adding Miss Denine as his confidant had not improved his accommodations, what it had done was allow him the chance to get Miss Denine and the bishop together. He was headed to the cathedral and while Father Young was unaware what to do once Miss Denine got to the cathedral, he was sure getting her there was essential. His mind pondered how to get her there again and again.

How to accomplish this had just come to him when he realized that it came with a price. Thinking of playing matchmaker, he had neglected the more pressing situation of his stomach and the bile in his throat was making him all too aware of the neglect. He willed his insides to remain just that, but it was too late. The contents of his stomach now joined him as an unwanted guest in his humble abode.

Behind the cathedral was an old barn that the last bishop had used to keep horses, sheep, and some other small animals. Bishop Goldheart had realized early on that caring for both horses and his drinking habit was impossible, so the barn was deserted. The empty barn still stood behind the cathedral or, at least, kind of stood behind the cathedral. Only half of the boards were still in place. Leftover hay and manure provided what little structural support remained.

Miss Denine pulled the wagon inside the back courtyard, hoping to avoid the female guards that sat in front of the cathedral hoping to follow in Mary's footsteps when it came to bagging a member of the cloth.

Miss Denine popped open the top of the keg once they were safely in the barn. Vomit and Father Young rolled out. Years of managing a tavern had made Miss Denine immune to the sight and smell of most bodily fluids.

"Sorry about the ride, but we seem to have made it safe and without detection," Miss Denine said proudly. She had always heard stories of people being smuggled by keg and dreamed one day she'd do it. Now she had. The fact that her passenger was a little worse for wear was not going to distract her from the pride of the accomplishment.

As far as safe and undetected went, Father Young would have liked to debate the definition of the word "safe" but the more obvious error in the statement was "undetected," for standing behind the beaming Miss Denine was Bishop Goldheart who had seen the carriage arrive from his back window. Upon seeing Miss Denine en route to his barn, the bishop went out in time to witness Miss Denine free Father Young from the keg.

"What is going on here?" was the bishop's rather reasonable question as he stood looking perplexed at the sight and smell of Father Young's emergence from the keg.

Miss Denine now turned and saw the bishop. Things betwixt the two were already a bit rocky and his questioning of her great accomplishment wasn't helping the situation, even if it was reasonable.

"Well, Bishop, glad to see you still live in town. I brought you Father Young as you seem unable to get him yourself."

The bishop opened his mouth, but nothing came out. Finally, he stuttered out. "I didn't even know Father Young needed getting gotten."

"Don't see how you would, given you never came by to check on him." Miss Denine paused for stinging effect, which proved very effective. "Well, safe and sound, delivered, one priest. I will be leaving you."

"One thing, Miss Denine," interrupted Father Young. This interruption was not like him. Rarely was he bold enough to interrupt, particularly given the tense conversation, let alone the fact that he was covered in vomit. But the ride had changed him. This plan had cost him dearly and he wasn't going to give it up now. Not only that, but he had also endured being jammed into a smelly keg only to avoid Mary and he decided if the cost of passiveness was so high, it was time to be a little more assertive.

"What, Father?" shot back Miss Denine who expected complaints about the ride.

"You have been so good to me this past while, and your food is exquisite. Would it be too much to ask you to stop by with a meal or two occasionally? At least while I hide from Mary?"

Miss Denine smiled, clearly a sucker for flattery, as she quickly said, "Of course, Father. At least someone feels my meals are worth asking for. In fact, if you want to visit every once and awhile, I could give you a ride in the keg. I always knew I could have made a good smuggler."

"No, thank you, just a meal now and again will be fine."

"Well then, I'll see you tomorrow," she said as she rode off.

Father Young had done it. Since the whole affair started, he had conceived various plans, but never actually put them into practice. He had finally spoken up and it had worked. Miss Denine was going to be back tomorrow. Although a bit battered and sitting there in his own vomit, he couldn't have been more pleased.

Chapter 16

The Damned Duke

Duke Diddlehop was duke of the region that included Lushton and Bridgecrest, but most of his time was spent in the courts of London. You might think that all dukes are short, fat, bald fops who spend all day seeking out gossip to share among the noble class. This prejudiced view did not apply to Duke Diddlehop. He was tall.

Currently, he was busy doing investigative work on Lord McElroy's latest affair. A fair man may say "alleged affair," but in London, among the nobles, the rule was simple—guilty until proven innocent and then, still probably guilty. Your best bet when caught in a scandal was to hope for, or create, a scandal involving someone in a higher station than you.

Hence, why Henry VIII had been so popular among the nobles. Under his rule you knew your scandal, no matter how large, was soon to be outdone by your king taking his wife's head off. Elizabeth was a different story, and while the "Virgin" Queen left speculation related to whom or when she might marry, the gossip around this was never sufficient to cover one's own scandals.

Diddlehop was extra anxious for information about Earl McElroy because the duke was rather on thin ice among the nobles and public opinion. He had been regent under the young King Edward and had been a significant part in many of the young king's religious reforms. But his mistake was in his defiance to recognize Queen Mary as legitimate heir to the throne. When the royal court had turned on him and accepted the new queen, he was lucky to escape with his head. In fact, the only way he was able to do so was by recanting the Church of England like no one had recanted before. He became more devoutly Catholic than the Pope. And while all this saved his royal backside, it made him look rather wishy-washy when Elizabeth came to the throne, and he was forced to recant his recanting. He was seen as fickle as Henry VIII choosing a bride. No one at court took him seriously. He needed more focus on someone or something else. And needed to convince the world that he was now solidly back into the Church of England.

And then, today, a new scandal. His sister was seen riding late at night with a peasant throwing rocks at Lord Whimple's large stained-glass window. True, the duke was so sick of Lord Whimple's bragging about that glass that he would have loved to see its demise, but his sister's involvement, especially with a peasant, was not helpful. To make matters worse, his sister's aim was no better than her judgment, so he had a scandal to deal with, and Lord Whimple still had his window.

True, Earl McElroy was merely an Earl, someone of lesser rank, but affairs, even as common as they were, held a special place in the rumor mill of London. He hoped it would be sufficient to cover for his and his sister's shortcomings.

To dig something up, the duke proceeded to make inquiries, much more to protect the family name than from any love of a sibling (truth was, she was only a half-sister, but he had already successfully covered up that scandal and would therefore rather I not mention it).

He was out scandal shopping today while at lunch with the Baroness of Newdell, his second cousin (some also believed she was another half-sister but let's stay focused on the scandal at hand).

The baroness was a close friend of Lady Firth, who was said to have been seen leaving Lord McElroy's house in the early hours of the morning less than a fortnight past. Diddlehop did not hope to find the blood-stained sword tip on his first try. No, he had played the game long enough to know that he was unlikely to string together enough pieces to ensure scandal on his first several visits. But if he could put Lady Firth near Lord McElroy's estate something around a fortnight ago, he would be well on his way. He didn't need the timeline to line up perfectly. Again, proof was not required, reasonable possibility would be enough.

The baroness was announced and Diddlehop stood. What followed next would take too long to articulate, but butlers bowed, people were announced, heads bobbed, rings, hands, cheeks and other things were kissed. At long last all sat, the hors d'oeuvres arrived, and Diddlehop's true work began.

"Baroness, your gardens look exquisite." Diddlehop threw this out, despite having not paid the slightest attention to the gardens.

"Oh, I hardly notice them anymore," she responded. His comment had the desired effect. She tried not to show it, but as he knew, the gardens at Durly, her estate, were her pride and joy. Usually this would be the beginning of much small talk, but Diddlehop had reason to hurry. He knew that if he stayed too long, she would be obligated to invite him for dinner, and he disliked her cook. "So, Baroness, how is Lady Firth?" Every noble knew this question well. It was the universal way of saying, "I wish to get juicy gossip about said person."

As Diddlehop expected, the baroness shot back with the standard answer, "She is well, why do you ask?"

"Well, I hate to pry," all nobles did, yet it never seemed to stop them, "but I had heard some disturbing news." A dramatic pause was given in hopes the baroness might chime in. This was also standard. One could always hope that the other might admit to a scandal without ever having to mention it, or mistakenly mention a separate scandal that they were unaware of. She sat attentively, clearly leaving the onus of the conversation on him.

"I would never be one to spread bad news." It is always a good idea to tell people you would never do the thing you are about to do. It builds credibility. "But I feel you, being such a close friend, should know, and perhaps could help clear her name, as I am sure it is not true."

"Duke, please speak plainly, we have no need to dance around the point. What is it my friend is supposed to have done?"

Normally Diddlehop liked to proceed more gingerly, but he was in a hurry. He could whiff the cook's dinner and did not smell any improvement since his last encounter. He lowered his voice. "Well, I have heard that she was seen with Lord McElroy at questionable hours about a fortnight ago."

"Duke Diddlehop, worry your mind no further regarding Lady Firth." The baroness's answer was quick and sure. Diddlehop did not like where this was going. "Lady Firth was with me and my Aunt Agatha for the past month. She and I only returned last Thursday. She ate with me nightly. However, it might interest you to know, while there, we found out that my aunt's priest is to marry." The ability to shut down Diddlehop and fit in her own news left her with a smile. She was so pleased with herself that she almost forgot to add salt to the fresh wound. Luckily years of practice paid off and she remembered to add in, "I wouldn't waste time chasing shady rumors, my friend."

All the nobles wasted time chasing shady rumors, but hated getting caught doing so, almost as much as they loved pointing out when others did. So, with his tail betwixt his legs, the duke began the ritual nobles went through to leave one another's presence. The description of this would be given if there was any hope that it could be understood, but even Duke Diddlehop, who was going through it, had no idea why he did what he did. All he knew was that it had to be done. Finally, he finished bowing and bobbing and made his exit.

Entering his carriage, his mind was in a frail state. Pride was a noble's most treasured limb and his had been wounded badly, but he also left with not even a whiff of scandal. If there had been a priest's wedding announced, then every noble would have been informed. The fact he had not heard about it reiterated how much respect he had lost since his days as regent.

Since Article 32 had been published, the only topic hotter than nobles' scandals, was the potential of priests to marry. The nobles all wanted their priest to be the first. The novelty of it was enough to excite them but it had the added benefit that it showed their allegiance to the changes the queen was making. Most were even chasing news of their priests being seen with or talking to women. The biggest disappointment among the nobles was how slow these priests seemed to be. They, having spent their lives chasing women, both before and after marriage, couldn't fathom what was taking these lifelong celibates so long.

None of this helped Diddlehop. He still had no scandal and was too far from his land to find out about his priests' love life. There was some thought of going to Lushton to find out if any of his priests were being chased by cupid. But nobles like him who had far-off land, and who pursued such information often turn up with nothing more than a month away from court to show for it. And a month of uncurtailed rumors can be dangerous and difficult to clean upon return, a headache Diddlehop could not afford at this time.

Despair seemed to overshadow everything in his life as he walked from his carriage to his home in London. As the front door opened, inside stood a page. *What now?* he wondered as he was handed a rough paper.

He paid the page and took the scroll. A part of him almost threw it away. The paper was clearly old, the corners frayed and stained. He shuddered to think where it had been. Worst of all it bore no seal or wrap. It had not come from a noble or at least not a noble with any nobility, which, of course, simply meant money. If any other noble had been watching, he would have seethed and thrown the scroll in the fire without opening it. He knew he was above this document, but he was alone, so he indulged his curiosity.

Dear Honorable Duke Diddlehop

He unrolled the parchment gingerly, with obvious disgust. This was undoubtedly from a quasi-literate peasant or his brother Andrew. Very few nobles wrote so poorly and if they did, they paid someone else to write for them. So, while it disgusted him that a peasant would write to him, it did increase his curiosity. He read on.

I am Henry of Bridgecrest. You are aware that due to us being Angelcans, priests can get wed. As duke over Bridgecrest, it may interest you that the priest of our town is doing that to Mary of Lushton.

No signature, no ending. Diddlehop quickly threw the paper in the fire and swore to himself that he would never admit where the information had come from, but as the paper burned, he smiled. Because while he would not admit to the information's origin, he most definitely was not above using it. He quickly gathered some much nicer parchment and his seal and started to write.

Dear Father Young, Priest of Bridgecrest

Chapter 17

Merry Messengers

"*O*ff to feed the pigs again?" Peter asked Fannie as she skipped across the road. Even though he could have answered his own question, it was the simplest way to start a conversation.

"Someone has to feed them while Father Young is away," Fannie replied.

"I have heard Father Young's doing quite well."

"What have you got for news about Father Young?" she said a little too quickly.

Peter noted the quick response in regards to news about Father Young. Over the past few days, they had crossed paths regularly, he running messages and her off to feed Father Young's growing herd. Somehow, they always got to the topic of Father Young, but it seemed to Peter it was in passing, rather something to fill up space, rather like potatoes on a plate, rather than the actual reason for the conversation. "I haven't heard a whisper about Father Young," was how he was forced to answer in the past, but now that he had news, her reaction was that of flies to fecal matter.

While he attempted to detect the motive for such excitement, Fannie's patience waned. "What have you heard about the father?" she demanded. The news about Article 32 was not limited to Lushton;

indeed, all of England was abuzz with females trying to snatch up monks, priests, bishops, and archbishops. While the news in Bridgecrest, like everywhere else, had spread, perhaps the only thing that kept the hysteria to a small simmer was the fact that there was not a priest to be snatched.

In fact, many women were sure that if only Father Young had been paying closer attention to his duties and been at home, they would have already been wed. Therefore, it was not difficult for Peter to determine the reason for Fannie's interest in Father Young. He had always viewed Fannie as more levelheaded than the average member of her sex. Only yesterday he had said to himself, after hearing a maiden describe to her associates the type of corset she would need once Father Young bought her a dress following their wedding, that the fairer sex all seemed at a loss to grasp the fact that there were hundreds of them in Bridgecrest and only one Father Young.

Indeed, the whole science of probability seemed to escape their grasp, but not so with Fannie, he'd thought. She's sane and practical. But now, seeing Fannie's grasp of the subject was so completely on par with that of her fellow maids, he now wrote off the sex entirely. The probability that even one female understood probabilities had sunk to zero. "So, you, like every other woman in town, fancy yourself to be Mrs. Young and feed them pigs the rest of your life, eh?"

Fannie did not expect Peter to quickly guess her secret. It was true, ever since she had heard of Article 32, she knew that fate had found a way. It hurt her to hear the other women in town talk of her Father Young, for she had loved and nursed him before loving a priest was fashionable. Hers was not a love based on money nor fame nor new corsets but a true love, and to hear Peter put it on the same level as those Jezebels struck her as unseemly. Her pride would not take it. So, looking rather hurt, she said a line that would be so insightful that in a short time it would become cliché, "None of your business."

"Well, you might be interested in the news I have, which is my business."

"Not in the least, you can have your news and take it to the grave."

This, of course, was a lie. She was dying to hear anything of the father. Every day she went to feed his pigs and watched the road, anxious for his return. While I don't wish to bore the reader with math, it is important to note that she had run into Peter regularly. While Peter frequented the road, you do not need to be a genius at probabilities to figure that the chances of Fannie running into him only going to feed pigs once a day were slim. Their meetings were so frequent because she was watching the road for the father. She would watch until Peter came along and said, "Hello, are you feeding the pigs again?" Then she'd say she was and walk on as if he just happened to catch her as she was walking back to the pigs. Peter should have realized this, but his grasp on probabilities did not much exceed his own assessment of the fairer sex's. I will now leave math behind and promise to leave it there. Getting back to the point at hand, which is, Fannie would do anything to know about Father Young . . . except allow damage to her pride, so she let Peter and his news walk off.

Peter was quite sure that in a few steps she would come running to his side, whimpering and sorrowfully admitting she was wrong for being so upset and that she'd do anything if he'd tell what he knew. It happened time and time again. He smiled as he walked away, anticipating the predicted events. But as her distance increased, his smile diminished. In time, he was forced to admit he had either underestimated Fannie's strength or overestimated the value of the news he had.

As it turns out, neither was true. The news' value could not have been higher and while strong as she was, her strength was not sufficient to go without the news. Where Peter had failed was in this female's grasp of probability. I know, I promised to leave math, but indulge me a little further. I honestly didn't think the subject would be important again, but well, it is. See, Fannie knew if Peter had news, there was a high probability that he had told others or that others had told him. Therefore, he was likely not the only source that could feed her yearning for the desired news. Therefore, in a dead sprint she ran to the back of the church, fed the pigs, and then dashed into town. No doubt, at such a pace mud was reaching high into her undergarments far further than it is appropriate for anything, even mud, to reach, but she didn't care. She had to know what news was available about Father Young.

Just as she was reaching her stride, she caught a glimpse out of the corner of her eye, a cottage. On that cottage porch she saw a man sitting. She was considerably more gifted in the mental regions than

Mary, yet as the speed of her legs went up, the speed of her brain went down. They were, as some might say, inversely proportional but I of course would not use such language.

She traveled about a hundred yards past the cottage in question before she remembered the cottage was Henry's and that the man sitting on the porch was the owner of the cottage. She stopped her dead sprint, let her mind and breath catch up, and slowly turned around. If anyone had news, it would be Henry. He always knew everything worth telling and plenty of things that weren't.

And indeed, she was right. He had only returned from Lushton that very morning. He was in fact Peter's informant, and a more direct source of misinformation would have been impossible to find.

She walked back briskly toward the cottage. She was as anxious as ever, but realizing she was being watched slowed her down.

"Good day, Henry."

"Good day, Miss Fannie. I couldn't help but notice your brisk pace a minute ago. Is everything okay?" Henry hoped that this would lead to more news. After all, someone at that pace could be coming from a fire, someone's death, or any number of wonderful things. Recently he had been on a bit of a rally and hoped it would continue.

"Oh, just . . . out for a bit . . . of exercise," she sputtered out between deep breaths. Henry didn't know what exercise was but did recognize that newsworthy it was not. Fannie tried to determine the best way to lead into what she was after, but having rarely conversed with Henry, she couldn't think of a starting point, so she went for the direct approach.

"Hear anything about Father Young?"

Poor Fannie, if she only knew, that was the only thing she could say to not get the information that she wanted about Father Young.

If she would have said, "Nice weather we are having," Henry would have said that it didn't compare to Lushton where he had just been and that while he was there, he had found the most interesting thing about Father Young. Or if she had said, "I hate broccoli," he would have said, "You know now that you mention it, broccoli reminds me about the father . . ." Henry enjoyed nothing in the world more than telling others about Father Young. Indeed, he had been on a bit of a tour the last few days stopping throughout Lushton and

Bridgecrest doing just that. However, since she wanted to know, he thought he better get something for it.

"Yes, Father Young. Many people seem to be asking about good old Father Young."

"So, do you have any news?"

"Can anyone really call it news?" Henry's attempts at being philosophical always fell short, and this left Fannie totally perplexed.

"Is he doing better?"

Now it was Henry's turn to be perplexed, for while in Lushton he was so caught up with who was with Father Young that he had failed to notice the obvious signs of struggle that were still rather vivid on his face. Therefore, he had no indication that he had ever been in a low enough state that people would care if he was any better. But he supposed someone might say, "Life is better with a woman at your side than without it," so he said, "Oh, he is better."

"So, he's talking again?"

"I'd say he is talking as well as he ever has." But with this Henry felt that Fannie was driving the conversation far too much, something he preferred to do, so he added, "Have you slaughtered any pigs lately?"

"Oh, yes, just yesterday." She too could play this game and before Henry could even think up any more questions about pigs, she asked, "Can he walk?"

"Yes, he can. Was it a big pig?"

"Fairly. How was his eye?"

"Fine. Have you eaten the rump?"

"Pa saves it for last. Did he seem upbeat?"

"I'd say. Are you willing to give me a healthy slice?"

This last question caught her off guard, which is exactly what Henry had hoped for. Up to this point his questions were simply small talk about pigs, designed to distract her from discussing Father Young. But now she realized, it was more. He was trying to work out terms. She wanted information and he wanted payment in the form of the hindquarters of the most recently departed member of the Porkshire household. "You want me to give you some pork, so you'll tell me about Father Young?"

Henry did not like the tone of the words or the accusation. However, he did like the proposition. Like most underhanded agreements, he knew that all it needed was the proper framing. "No, all I am saying is that there have been so many people asking about the father that I have grown hungry by the telling and retelling of the tale. One might even call me famished. So, if I had the promise of a good meal to sustain me, I might be able to gather the energy required to tell this tale one more time."

"All right, tell me what you know, and I'll give you the pork."

Henry smiled and prepared to tell his tale. Practice was his ally. Every hand motion, voice inflection, and dramatic pause was memorized. He gave a flawless performance, but Fannie did not notice. Father Young, Mary, and a kiss had been muttered far too close together. It couldn't be. How could he? This was unfair and she knew it. How could she expect him to know how she felt, or why should she assume he cared for her? All she knew was that she was supposed to be his and he hers and fair or not she wished he'd act like it.

Act II was beginning, but Fannie could hear no more as the silent pantomime continued amid the deafening clamor of her storm-filled mind. She knew only one thing, she wished for solitude. Her mind groped for an excuse to run away. But before any words could form, the billowing clouds of mental anguish began to release their torrent. A greater downpour than Bridgecrest had received in a fortnight began to flow. Under such circumstances, Fannie found it difficult to excuse herself, so she didn't. She just ran, leaving a healthy trail of tears behind her.

Chapter 18

An Aggressive Suitor

Many women have wept and bemoaned their life when they have found themselves married to a drunk. If they only knew what the first few months of sobriety were like, the next few drinks would be on them. Or, at least, that is what Father Young thought as he had to listen to Bishop Goldheart go on endlessly about the good old days and how things used to be.

True, the tavern had turned into a prison for Father Young after Fannie's departure. The daring barrel escape had left him with hope of sanctuary, but this cathedral was not being too sanctuary-ous. The cathedral, Father Young had thought, would lead to more freedom simply because of its number of exits. Miss Denine's bar had two and the cathedral had five. True, two of these were on the same side so they could be viewed by one individual, but with four options and only one Mary, Father Young assumed he'd have favorable odds at getting a free escape. So, while three of four sounds good, it did not account for the fact that Mary or more likely her mother had enlisted help and formed Mary and Associates. The company's sole goal was a merger with Father Young.

Father Young couldn't be sure, but after a few days he was fairly confident Mary and Associates was a group of three, Mary herself, her mother, and her most valued employee, Peter the messenger boy. For Peter, work had been slow in Bridgecrest, and he was sick of secondhand stories about Father Young. For a messenger boy, Article 32 was like striking gold, yet Peter was smart enough to know that his gossip mining claim was in Lushton and after his talk with Fannie, he decided he should go work it. And work it he did. Within a few hours of arrival, he had contacted Mary and joined the firm. He quickly became its highest paid employee. So, while the growth of Mary and Associates may have been good news for the stock portfolio, it was not good news for the father's chances of a quiet walk without a blonde on his right arm. One out of four was not good odds and Peter's speed made the odds even less than that.

With the trepidation of a lamb needing to cross a lion's den, Father Young would attempt to sneak out whenever he could stand the bishop's company no more. If he chose Mary's exit, her gleeful laugh would let him know rather quickly that he had once again chosen and lost. "Oh Father, so good to see you. Where shall we go today?" she would say as she grabbed his arm.

One time she had made the mistake of squealing too soon, thereby giving Father Young ample time to shuffle back into the cathedral before his arm was taken hostage. A mistake not to be repeated.

If the mother's exit was chosen, shortly after walking out, a scurry in the bush would be heard, and a scampering mother would be seen, and Father Young knew Mary was soon to follow. One time, he had tried to out-scurry the mother and Mary, but Father Young had found them to be very effective scurriers.

Peter was a very different story. Father Young liked Peter. Peter was no fool. Given how anxious Mary was for a lookout, he knew Father Young must be less keen than the gossip chain was reporting. The first time Peter saw Father Young trying to escape unaccompanied, he casually began speaking to the father and essentially guided him until they ran into Mary, and that is how he discovered whose side Peter was on. So, it was with sorrow that today, as Father Young slunk out of the cathedral, that no more than ten feet from the door, he heard Peter's voice behind a large buttress.

"Morning, Father."

"Good morning, Peter."

"So, Father, out for a walk?" Peter asked.

Father Young thought briefly, he had no desire for Peter to lead him to Mary again, so said, "No, just seeing how the weather is today. Then I'm going back into the cathedral," Father Young tried.

"Listen Father, I know you don't want to see Mary. I hate to turn you over to her, Father, but a job is a job," Peter said with a wink.

Father Young didn't understand why Peter was winking. He was glad to hear that Peter didn't enjoy turning him over, he didn't see how sympathy was going to help, and the truth was that sympathy alone wasn't. All Father Young gave Peter was a blank stare.

"Father, I don't like giving you up to Mary, but I have to. After all, what kind of man would I be if I didn't honor a paying customer?" Peter was convincing, and Father Young was resigned to another walk with Mary. "Then again, if I had a separate paying customer who asked me not to deliver you to Mary, then the decision would not be so simple." Peter again winked.

Father Young saw how this would add an ethical wrinkle to the situation, but as a priest, he dealt more with pretty cut-and-dry sins, so he was no master of ethics or suggestion for that matter.

"You see what I am saying, another, different paying customer." Peter tried the wink one last time, but Father Young's stare was as blank as ever. "Father, give me six brass, and you're free to go."

Suddenly, Father Young understood, Peter's job as agent was lucrative but the job of double agent was doubly so. The ethics might still be questionable but before Father Young could feel any guilt, he handed Peter his ransom. "Father, I'd appreciate it if you reentered by this door as I'll be sure it's mine to watch," he heard Peter request as he continued. Father Young turned and gave a nod. Then he happily headed down the trail leading down the back of the cathedral following a cool brook.

The morning was an excellent one. Flowers had begun to pop up on the skirts of the brook. Father Young had always admired the brook as an oasis amid Lushton. He loved the life that clung to its banks, refusing to be squelched out by the dusty path that encroached from both sides.

Father Young thought of how this brook gave so much life. Yet the brook, the very life blood of all around it, was the same thing that had attracted people to settle in Lushton, the same thing that brought the roads, the buildings, the cars, pigs, and people that had removed so much of the life that had once surrounded this brook. With regard to the grass and the trees, the brook both gave and took life.

The Church, Father Young felt, had done much the same in his life. Everything his life was, was because of the Church. His living, his job, his associations, all came because of the Church. It, like the brook, had caused him to flourish. Yet it had kept him from love, something, until recently, he thought little about, but now it seemed a most vital part of his life. Now, the Church had reversed its stance. Yet again, his association with the Church made his hand desirable and Father Young was discovering that the more desired one's hand, the harder it seemed to acquire a suitable companion.

The analogy twisted through Father Young's mind and in one twist, a connection was made. The mind has a way of folding, twisting, altering the strangest connections, but he realized that for plants, at least, life or death depended a great deal on proximity to the brook. Plants directly over the brook survived, while those just a cubit away, were stamped out by passing carts.

He had forgotten exactly what the brook was in the analogy. Was it the Church or his chance at happiness, which he now equated with love, which equaled Fannie? Either way his church and Fannie were both in Bridgecrest and he was here. Proximity was the key and in that, he was failing.

Before the reader spends any length of time analyzing this analogy, please remember that Father Young was in love. Analogies discovered in love often resemble those found while drunk or at 2 a.m.

Suddenly, he asked himself a clear and obvious question, *Why are you still in Lushton?* Somehow the oppressive confines of the company he kept of late had clouded his mind but now under the trees and sunlight he could clearly see. *Why had he not left sooner?* he asked himself. All he could even think was holding him back was that first, he wanted to see Miss Denine and the bishop together, and second, he still felt unwell. On the first count, Miss Denine had again come the next day to visit the cathedral, but on that occasion, Father Young might as well have been a pitcher of water at a wedding. The bishop and Miss Denine had so quickly stocked up a conversation and were so absorbed with each other that neither would have noticed his absence. The matchmaking had quickly reached a significant flame that it no longer needed a match. On the second count, Father Young had truly felt himself still ill. But now he realized it was simply the sickness of captivity and Mary, for he was always stricken with one or the other. Freedom had cured him.

Realizing that to stay another day—even another moment—in Lushton was foolishness, Father Young marched back to the cathedral.

He was happy to see Peter at his previous post. Peter smiled to see Father Young. "Glad you know how to follow good advice."

"Peter," said Father Young, ignoring the fact that Peter's advice had nothing to do with it, "I wish you to escort me back to Bridgecrest without Mary knowing."

Peter began to interject something about his need to be loyal to those who employed him, but Father Young was prepared and knew all about Peter's loyalties, so before Peter could start, Father Young said, "I will pay you ten brass. So, plan our escape while I go say good-bye to the bishop."

Peter's demeanor portrayed that he was ready to obey more than words could, but with ten brass on the line, he didn't want any misinterpretation. "Yes sir, I await your command."

After a short goodbye to the bishop, Father Young was out on his way. Peter and Father Young could not make their way directly back to Bridgecrest as the direct route would have likely taken them past Mary or others in Mary and Associates. Unfortunately, the next most direct path was not a path at all. Much of what the two engaged in over the next hour or so is what many call bushwhacking, but in reality, the more descriptive word to describe it would be stupid. Peter did not mind bushwhacking, or any other sport for that matter. Father Young, on the other hand, disliked sports and bushwhacking particularly at this moment. However, he realized the need to avoid people. Mary and Associates was not the only thing to avoid. Any eye that caught sight of him had a chance to become a mouth that might take word of his departure back to Mary. Father Young did not wish for Mary and Associates to move headquarters. Indeed, his church in Bridgecrest only had two exits, three with the hole, but Mary could easily see Father Young leave with a single view. Yes, if the cathedral had been a prison, then the church would be a cage. The longer word of his exit was delayed in Lushton, the better. Plus, time would be needed if he was to win Fannie, something difficult to accomplish with a different girl on your arm.

Indeed, Father Young had hoped to use the walk to Bridgecrest to cultivate an idea for the wooing of young Miss Porkshire. However, each time the beginnings of a plan would creep into his cranium, a maple branch landed in the same location. Indeed, branches of all sorts seemed in a race with his thoughts and the branches were coming off victorious. Warding off the branches, Peter held back only to release when in perfect alignment with his face and planning his eternal bliss was simply incompatible.

"Peter, perhaps we should head back to the trail?" Father Young suggested, panting heavily.

"Well, do you want someone to see us?"

"At some point someone will, but I cannot go on like this. Plus, eventually Mary will assume me dead or escaped anyway and, at that point, all we can do is make time."

Peter shrugged, turned, and headed back to the path. Once there, their pace increased considerably. Even at such a pace, Father Young could think again, and the more he thought, the more hopeless he became. Winning Fannie's affection was never his strong suit. He had had many occasions to do it before and all had ended the same. Not to mention an earlier thought kept ringing in his mind. *It will be difficult to woo Fannie on your right arm if Mary's on your left.* Even if Matthew said you could keep the right hand from knowing what the left was doing. How long could he reasonably expect to avoid Mary? His escape would be common knowledge in a day or two at best, and Mary was sure to follow. Of all her faults, and Father Young could list many, quitting easily was not one of them. He had done nothing to be rid of Mary. His freedom was fleeting, and he knew it. This became a circle of thoughts that spun around in his brain until one fell out his mouth. "How am I to get rid of Mary?" The question had been directed at himself and was rhetorical in nature, but Peter was not one for rhetoric, so he assumed it had been addressed to him.

The question was a simple one and in Peter's mind, had a simple answer. When a man did not want a woman who wanted him, it was his duty to tell her off. But while Peter saw the simplicity of the answer, he saw the difficulty of the situation. He knew the father and because of the father's goodness, even Peter could see that he lacked the needed disposition to properly tell off anyone, let alone a beautiful young lady. For, in the formidable years, when men and boys like Peter were learning real skills, like how to pop someone in the nose, or properly tell someone off, poor Father Young was wasting his time with fasting, cleaning, reading, and writing. As well as I could make a man a playwright in a day, Peter could make Father Young a real man in one walk to Bridgecrest.

Just because Father Young knew little and needed much, would Peter not teach him? Did a young man like Peter let what seemed impossible stop him? Yes. He stalled while he thought of a plan to rid Father Young of Mary that would not require the father to grow a backbone.

"Why do you want to get rid of Mary?" Peter asked, stalling for time.

"Well, she is everywhere, she wants to be with me all the time. I'd rather . . ." Father almost said *be with a different woman*, but caught himself, " . . . be left alone" he finished.

"Oh, I know she's a bit annoying, always wanting to be by your side, but if it wasn't her, it would simply be another woman who flung herself at you. Why not just let her hang there?" Peter said, gesturing to the father's arm.

Father Young's arm shuddered as the memory of her favorite attachment point was still fresh. "Peter, I hope it's not true. If every woman was as Mary, it would be awful. I'd never have any peace."

"I'm afraid it is, Father. I once thought that there must be one sensible female out there, just one, but I am afraid it is a lost cause. Do you want to know how I know?"

It was interesting to have this young boy, no more than sixteen years, giving lessons to a priest, but if asked, Father Young would have likely acknowledged Peter's superior knowledge on all things female and therefore he simply nodded to his question.

"Well, you know Mr. Porkshire? I've seen you talk to him often."
Another nod.

"You may not have noticed, but he has a daughter. Her name is Fannie."

Air went down the wrong pipe and Father Young coughed and sputtered.

"You okay, Father?" Peter said as he stopped and allowed Father Young to catch up.

"Sorry about that, just . . . well it doesn't matter, you were saying something about Fannie?"

"Yes, well, she is the most level-headed female that I know, and even she fancies marrying you."

Father Young again swallowed down the wrong pipe, much worse this time, and began frantically coughing as his mind tried to keep him alive while he processed what Peter just said. Father Young, breathing again, took the words apart, and put them back together to ensure he didn't miss a not, or a no, or any other simple word that would alter the meaning, and then asked, "What?"

"Yes, it shocked me too, Father," Peter said as he again began walking. "But as you can see, sensible females do not exist, and if it's not Mary, it will be some other broad at your side."

Father Young ignored Peter's higher point on women and sensibility and tried to push Peter back to specifics on Fannie as he followed in Peter's steps. "How do you know Fannie wishes to marry me, Peter?"

"Father, you're missing the point. It's not about Fannie." Peter stopped and looked Father Young in the eyes. "Don't you get it? They all want to marry you. You have money and power. Even if you don't use either all that well, you got 'em, and they want 'em."

Father Young was not going to let this go. "How do you know Fannie Porkshire particularly wishes to marry me?"

Peter paused as he looked up and scratched his chin. "Well . . . .she mentioned it, or something sort of like it, I think. When she was off feeding your pigs."

Despite the bad news that someone was feeding his pigs, Father Young's eyes grew bright and his smile wide. "She told you that she wanted to marry me." Father Young turned to continue his journey to Bridgecrest as he continued to mutter under his breath, "She wants to marry me . . . Me. Fannie Porkshire, actually wants me."

Clearly for some reason outside of Peter's grasp, the father loved Fannie. He did not see anything wrong with her, but two moments ago he'd felt it unlikely that the father had even known she existed. Peter allowed Father Young to walk ahead alone as he sat and thought. Father Young clearly didn't notice Peter stop and Peter was sure he'd get safely back home without him. Peter turned and headed back to Lushton. He had a job to do.

Chapter 19

A Priest's Confession

ather Young's plan had been to instantly head to the Porkshire's cottage, ask for Fannie's hand and propose, but by the time he had made it to the church, night had fallen and he determined it was too late. But first thing in the morning he would be on his way to the Porkshires'. However, now the sun had risen, but his confidence had not. In the light of a new day, all seemed bleak again. Somewhere between hearing of Fannie's love and all his self-made merriment, he had forgotten that despite her love, he still had to talk to her, something he had failed to do up to this point.

It had played over and over in his mind last night. He would walk up to her, stare into her big brown eyes, and she would know. Somehow she would know that he knew of her love and she would also see in his eyes the love he had for her. A warm embrace would follow, full of joy and relief. But upon waking up this morning, he had realized that giving a stare that says, "I love you and I know you love me too," was a bit difficult to pull off.

Now, looking in the mirror, he thought his best attempt may be confused for the "I know I should know your name, but I can't recall it just now" stare. And, if the stare should fail, he knew that words would be required, so what could he say? "Listen, I know you love me." He doubted that was the right thing, and now, he doubted even that, the one fact that had led to all this. Could he really trust Peter? What if Peter had misheard her? At the time he had been so utterly happy that he didn't ask for details. Perhaps, Peter had heard it in a dream, or he was thirty feet away, half listening in. Perhaps, she said it in an attitude of mocking other girls. What had been yesterday's facts were today's doubts.

If only he had known Peter's plan, then he really would have been dismayed. For Peter had left with every intention of helping Father Young, but unfortunately, ran into a man who was willing to pay in cold hard coin for his message and helping the father only meant blessings in the life to come, and Peter realized a bird in the hand . . .

Luckily for Father Young, there was one factor that made today different from the previous, and that was Mary. Because of her, the clock was ticking, and action was required. She may be on the path to Bridgecrest at this very moment. This fact alone forced his doubts to the side and had propelled him down a familiar path to the Porkshires'.

Mary was not on the path to Bridgecrest. Rather, she was at a meeting of Mary and Associates. Her mother had heard a traveler tell of a priest singing and dancing towards Bridgecrest. They were discussing what was to be done. Perhaps discussing is not the optimum term, for it amounted to sobs from one and consoling comments from the other during breaths.

Mary thought she had lost her prey. Her mother, on the other hand, had not given up. Finally, as Mary's sobs softened, her mom spoke.

"Mary didn't you hear Father Young was dancing and singing? He was excited," she said with a smile.

"So!"

"What could be more exciting than an engagement?"

As tears slowed, she asked, "What engagement?"

"Why, to you, of course."

"But we're not engaged."

"Not yet of course, he had to go to Bridgecrest to work out the arrangements before his engagement."

Tears and sobs were becoming less frequent. "You think he's going to come back and propose?"

"Of course, he is! The way he's spent every minute he can with you, what else would he do? Now we'd better be ready. Perhaps we will ask the tailor to start getting your dress ready, and the flower man to get bouquets."

"But we can't tell anyone until he asks?" Mary questioned.

"Oh, you're right, dear, but I'm sure he'd want us to be ready. I'll tell you what. How about everyone you tell that you're engaged to Father Young, you have them promise not to tell anyone." When it came to marketing, Mary's mother was a wonder.

"Great idea, Mom!" Mary clearly felt lying, if done hypocritically, by telling others not to do the same, was okay.

"Once we get things ready, we'll go and surprise him in Bridgecrest."

The path between Lushton and Bridgecrest was well worn. Almost anyone from Bridgecrest who could spare the time had traveled to Lushton to gain any news possibly related to Article 32. And indeed, Henry was just such a traveler. After the wild success of his last trip to Lushton, he had enjoyed numerous speaking engagements, but Bridgecrest is not large and sadly Henry had run out of people to tell, so spurred by his recent success in procuring a port haunch, back to Lushton he went in search of his next gem.

The Porkshire's humble wooden front door again found itself in a staring match with Father Young. Over the past few months, Father Young had often found himself frozen in front of this door. The door was confused, most people seemed to know what to do when they met him. They smack him a few times in the face and someone else would grab him by the rear and thrust him open. Such was the life of a door, and the custom was fairly universal, except when the father came to him.

Father Young seemed to be unaware of the need to smack him in the face to queue others to grab his rear. Instead, the father would stand looking petrified until someone would grab the rear and surprise them both. One would think the door would have been happy with this arrangement. After all, the only thing it left out was a few steady smacks to the face, but the door was not happy. The normal ritual gave the door warning. Now he was left in suspense. True, doors often get grabbed in the rear without warning, but that's just it: either there was no warning or there was a direct warning. Father Young put the door in a strange middle ground that he was not comfortable with. Father Young stood staring at him, so he knew that soon someone was going to grab him from behind. Yet without the father to cue in this someone, there was no telling when they'd do it. How would you feel staring down one assailant knowing at any moment another would grab you from behind? So, the two sat, each just as uncomfortable as the other. Until Mr. Porkshire grabbed his rear and thrust him open.

Mr. Porkshire now found himself with the same view the door had: a very uncomfortable Father Young. But Mr. Porkshire was accustomed to finding a nervous priest at his door. The extraordinary coincidence that the father always seemed to arrive just as Mr. Porkshire was leaving, leaving the former no time to knock did not bother Mr. Porkshire. After all, it was a coincidence, even if it was an extraordinary one. The expression of anxiety and fear that always accompanied the father's features, Mr. Porkshire had long ago decided was the expression of the anxious student ready for a lesson, and today was no different. "Ah, Father Young, now that your health is restored and you have come home, you wish to pick up where we left off?" The expression was articulated to sound like a question, but no time for response was given. "Let's see, last we met we were reviewing how to identify slop types by smell, I believe. Oh look, here is a great specimen."

Mr. Porkshire's lecture had begun. He took up a bucket and inhaled far deeper than most men could endure with a smell half so putrid. "That is . . . well, I shouldn't just give away the answer, you have had this lesson. Tell me, what do you think it is?" Mr. Porkshire said, as he handed the bucket to the father.

Mr. Porkshire was right. Father Young had indeed had the lesson, but right now the smell of slop and the memory of the smells from former lessons was not the only thing making him feel ill. It was the repetitive nature of it all. He had run from town to town, been beaten, ridden in a barrel of vomit, and endured Mary, all for Fannie, and to what avail? Here he was, exactly where he had started, sniffing pig slop at Porkshire Porcine University. The cycle had to stop. With all the strength of will he possessed, he stated, "No pigs today, Mr. Porkshire. I have come to speak with Fannie."

Mr. Porkshire did not usually take kindly to anyone saying "no" and "pigs" in the same sentence, let alone directly adjacent to one another. But Father Young had proven himself and his love of swine. Not only that, Mr. Porkshire was also curious. Why would Father Young want to speak with Fannie? As long as Mr. Porkshire had known the father, his sole interest in the Porkshires had been pork, as it should be. True, he had been willing to run to Lushton after Fannie. But surely, a sidekick helping a needy parent was just a good deed, or at least that is how Mr. Porkshire saw it. Amidst all the actions of Father Young, there had never been an apparent desire to see or talk to Fannie.

Mr. Porkshire was correct, but his error was that he assumed that actions matched intentions. A common enough mistake for any detective. Mr. Porkshire couldn't hide his surprise, much like an owner bitten by a loyal dog for the first time. You still love the dog but wonder why. But unlike a dog, which is rather difficult to gather information from, Mr. Porkshire realized that he could simply cure his curiosity with a question and so asked, "Why?"

Father Young hoped Mr. Porkshire would jaunt off and fetch Fannie. He could then see her beautiful face and awkwardly confess his love, but with this one word, Mr. Porkshire brought the awkwardness of the situation to the forefront. Lying, as demonstrated throughout his life, was one of Father Young's weakest points, and with little time to come up with a plan, he simply came clean. "Because, Mr. Porkshire, I love her."

If Mr. Porkshire had been surprised as the loving owner whose trusted dog bit him before, he now looked like the owner who found his dog had bit him and then as an encore ran off with his only daughter. Mr. Porkshire loved both Father Young and Fannie and was pleased, but like the dog owner didn't expect the two to be a match. So, despite his shock, the overwhelming emotion he felt was joy. It wasn't the joy that most parents would feel about learning their daughter had a rich suitor. Every master fears that their apprentice, after years of training in the great profession, will change career paths.

Mr. Porkshire knew that Father Young was, and always would be a priest, but secretly hoped that his true passion would become pigs. He assumed he could make it the case and being his father-in-law would be a perfect position to ensure that Father Young stayed under his tutelage. Not only this, but the whole Mason John affair was also not far out of Mr. Porkshire's mind. Marrying off his daughter had always been very far back in his mind, after all, she was still a piglet in his eyes. But John had moved the problem of finding a suitable mate from the back to the forefront of his mind. In recent days, it had even interrupted his thoughts as he was trying to focus on tending pigs. Father Young was suitable, indeed, compared to John, he appeared as suitable as Thomas Gunsal, the first recorded pig farmer in England, which of course, you already knew.

Mr. Porkshire's face relaxed, and he said, "Excellent, my boy, I'm glad to hear it." But no sooner had he expressed his joy in voice then his mind caught hold of some complications. Mary was the talk of the town, and even Mr. Porkshire, who avoided all gossip, had heard disgusting talks of warm embraces. So, Mr. Porkshire asked, "What about this Mary person from Lushton?"

Father Young's face instantly looked like one in pain. Her name alone was a weapon against him and the look on his face told Mr. Porkshire both that the father was not going to name his first-born daughter Mary and more importantly that he clearly did not love her. This made Father Young's next words unnecessary, but he stated emphatically, "I do not care for Mary. She is a leech."

Father Young's words shocked himself. He often thought about how many characteristics Mary shared with something that attaches to you and won't let go but did not ever expect himself to vocalize the comparison, especially so clearly.

Things were changing in Bridgecrest. Father Young, who had rarely felt the need to speak what he thought, was liking the outcomes. Now with Fannie's father's approval, he did not want to leave doubt about his views on Mary, and indeed all females not named Fannie Porkshire.

This settled the matter in Mr. Porkshire's mind. Others may worry about the court of public opinion, but with a love of pigs, mud, and research, Mr. Porkshire had decided long ago to ignore that court's rulings, and he did not plan to change the policy today. However, this did not end his doubts. Fannie's affections towards John had been hard for Mr. Porkshire to miss and he had seen no more signs of Fannie's love for Father Young than he had seen of the father's for Fannie. "Does Fannie love you?"

A clearly stated answer had worked well for Father Young previously but this question made his path forward much more complicated. He had no idea. He hoped Peter was correct, but hope was void of knowledge and Father Young could not even say he had faith on the subject. His honesty continued, "I have no idea."

"You haven't told her?" Mr. Porkshire asked honestly.

"No," Father Young said as his confidence visibly faltered.

Mr. Porkshire had grown to know Father Young well over the past few years. Both the problem and the solution were clear to him.

"Father, why don't you head home and look after your pigs." Mr. Porkshire thought that would relax him. "Leave the rest to me."

Chapter 20

A Talk with the Father

F annie," Mr. Porkshire called out, as loudly as was necessary in his one room shack. Fannie was sitting at the front table weaving a basket. She was surrounded by baskets on the table and all over the floor.

"Yes, Father?"

"We need to talk."

"Go ahead, Father."

Mr. Porkshire kicked baskets as he approached the table and then pushed a pile of them on the floor so that he could see Fannie as he spoke. "Was that Father Young?" she asked.

"Yes, it was and that was a bit of what I wanted to speak to you about." Mr. Porkshire, like all fathers, had a basic idea of what had to be said, but, like all fathers, had no idea how to say it. "Fannie, did you enjoy caring for Father Young?"

Fannie had no idea where this was going. She had spent the last few days torn between trying to forget Father Young and thinking of possible early demises for Mary. Therefore, while her mind had been busy, her bored hands had become jealous. To appease her uneasy limbs, she had taken to weaving baskets.

She did not want to hear about Father Young or talk about him, even if that was all she thought about, but despite all this, she was not one to lie so she said, "Yes, Papa, I enjoyed it."

"It was good of you to do. He is looking much better."

This news was, as all news about Father Young, two-edged. She was happy to know that the man she loved was doing better, yet she knew a piece of her felt differently. She felt her head grow hot and as she saw Father in the arms of Mary, she also envisioned what had occurred to Father just before he had been found beaten in the street and tried to stop her inner anger from wishing that it happen again.

"Fannie, have you thought about moving out on your own?"

"No." The reply came very quickly. Mr. Porkshire's face let her know the answer had been too fast to be believable. "Well," she admitted, "I've thought about it, but always as something that would happen far into the future. I like it here with you and Mom." Fannie had been forcing herself to believe this ever since she became aware of Mary.

"We like having you also." Mr. Porkshire's smile was as soft as the mud he so often worked in. "But a father can't keep his daughter forever."

"Are you trying to get rid of me?" Fannie said as tears began to well in her eyes. She hardly knew why she was crying, but she was. She didn't know where this was going, but she was suddenly overwhelmed with love for her father.

"Not unless it makes you happy," Mr. Porkshire said softly as he handed her a hankie, which had enough mud on it to make it useless.

The tears picked up. "Papa, what are you talking about?"

"Fannie, do you think you would want to care for Father Young for the rest of your life?"

She was now bawling, which confused Mr. Porkshire. He had no idea if things were going well or horribly. Both ways seemed to elicit the same result at times . . . bawling.

Fannie hardly knew what to say. Father Young was going to marry Mary but must have come to her papa requesting that she be brought on as a maid or something. No matter how much she loved him, she was not going to sit by and wait on him and Mary.

The fates that control our lives and work endlessly to ensure that good women and men never get together were laughing as Fannie prepared the next line, she was preparing to say, "I don't want to, I want to stay here." Of course, then Mr. Porkshire would assume that she didn't want to wed Father Young. The miscommunication and confusion that drives all good love stories would have gone on. But while the fates were laughing, they missed the slight change in Fannie's word choice and allowed her to blurt out. "I will never serve that woman."

Instantly, the fates stopped laughing and sat in silence, hoping Mr. Porkshire had not heard her, but it was not to be. He had heard, and quickly asked, "What woman?"

"Mary, of course," came her reply.

Suddenly, it was clear to Mr. Porkshire. The talk of Mary had reached Fannie. "No, no, no, my dear, Father Young loathes Mary."

This one sentence suddenly changed Fannie's whole outlook on life. One might ask why she was so sure that her papa was such an expert on Father Young's view of other women, but she was so anxious to believe him that she didn't question his authority on the subject. With her mental state quite changed, she quickly forgot about all the ill will she had once had for Father Young and Mary. Before sadness and anger had led her to tears, but now that she was elated, she quickly turned again to tears.

"Father Young does not want a maid. He won't need one because he wants a wife." Mr. Porkshire may have been progressive on his view of pigs but his views on the opposite sex were fairly grounded in the 1500's.

The tears continued to flow, far too much to allow Fannie to speak. She smiled at her father and took him in her arms in such a way that even Mr. Porkshire, a man, understood.

Chapter 21

The Wedding

ishop Goldheart awoke to the loud knock of a young page the morning after Father Young left. There was no doubt where this parchment had come from. The messenger alone had been enough proof. He was clearly a cut above the local messengers and looked more like a page from London than the messenger boys you got in such towns as Bridgecrest and Lushton. But the seal made it clear. Duke Diddlehop was up to something. It was the only reason one would hear from him or see his face in town. Underneath the seal were two pages, the first an official invitation, the other a personal letter. First, the invitation, which was made to look as fancy as possible, announced and invited the recipient to the marriage of Father Young of Bridgecrest and Mary of Lushton. The fact that Lushton had a handful of Marys had not worried the duke. After all, even if they grabbed the wrong one, his needs would still be met. The announcement included a long list of the nobles who had been invited to attend, far more than would fit in the small church at Bridgecrest. Diddlehop, having only set foot in the church when he was approximately three years old, seemed to remember the church as much larger than it was.

The most alarming part of the announcement was the date. The wedding was to take place the following day. The duke figured, the sooner the better, and would have held it sooner if he could have traveled and gotten the message out in time.

The next page was a personal note to Bishop Goldheart. It instructed him to make sure he would be at the church to perform the ceremony. The bishop was a little offended that he had been told, not asked, but knew his place when it came to the duke. He had no idea how all this had come about but knew it must be a mistake. However, mistakes among nobles were not easily corrected and never admitted. If Duke Diddlehop had told the nobles that Father Young was to marry Mary of Lushton then the bishop felt it likely that the following day Father Young would be marrying Mary.

The other issue was the time. This note had just arrived in Lushton, meaning that Father Young would likely not hear of this until the day of the wedding, Bridgecrest being a good distance further from London. This meant that he would have very little, if any, warning before his church was descended upon by the very dregs of London (commonly known as nobility) in order to see him marry a woman he despised. Pleading for the duke to have mercy would only fall on deaf ears. After all, marrying your enemies was just another day for most nobles.

Bishop Goldheart felt responsible for all this. After all, poor Father Young had made him a confidant early on and it left the bishop with the feeling that he should do something . . . but what? If he were to act, he would have to come up with a strategy on the road. He quickly packed and headed out the door.

His first glance of the roadway told Bishop Goldheart that he had not been the first to hear about the upcoming nuptials. The main square outside the cathedral, which was usually the most active part of town, looked like the plague had washed through with 100% success. He felt like an Israelite who had slept in on the day of the Exodus. All this simply meant he would have to pick up his pace. Hopefully, it would aid his ability to think.

Father Young waited at the church for news from Mr. Porkshire long into the night before finally falling asleep. When he awoke, he began to feel glummer. When Mr. Porkshire had said to leave everything to him, he had been happy to have the situation out of his hands and in someone else's. But at that time, he had no clue how hopeless sitting around hoping that others will take care of your problems can be. There he sat, staring down the path, hoping to see Mr. Porkshire come into view, hopefully with a smiling Fannie skipping at his side. While he didn't see Mr. Porkshire, he did note an awful lot of people coming from the other direction. Traffic on the small road to the church was usually only a few travelers an hour, but soon it turned into a steady flow. The strange part was he didn't see them on the other side of the road. He could not see the front of his church from his quarters in the back, but that was the only logical place all these people could be going. As he continued to watch, a most frightful sight caught his eye. Mary's mother, followed by Mary in a dress, not an ordinary dress, but one that one might wear for . . . he didn't dare say it, he didn't even dare think it, and directly behind the mother-daughter duo, an official-looking page.

The page, by all rights, should have been there last night, or much earlier this morning, but page boys cannot always be trusted, especially those from London. And the steady flow of alcohol he had received in Lushton for news of the wedding had left the trail between the towns a bit difficult to walk. This left ample time for all of Lushton to join him on the road. No one traveled with more happiness and glee than Mary's mother. After all, nothing brightens one's faith in fate so much as when you make up a lie and wake up to find it's true.

Soon the knock came. Father Young got up from his quarters and headed to the front of the church knowing it would do little good to try to ignore the page. The page would stay and knock until Father Young came to the door. The tumult outside made it clear most of both towns were out front. Upon opening the door a small crack, Mary practically tackled the page trying to force her way in as she smiled, gave a wave, and said, "Hello, Father, you are looking so bright today." Both she and her mother gave him looks of eager anticipation that made seeing them even scarier than he thought it would be.

The page straightened and pushed back Mary and handed him a scroll. Father Young took the scroll and quickly shut the door as Mary tried to advance to fill the void where the page had been.

Father Young opened the scroll and read the invitation to his wedding. Father Young's stomach churned, and his face felt flush. He had felt so confident it would all work out moments ago. But now, he was doomed. How could he refuse a duke? It was true that in the past few weeks he had grown some backbone, but having grown one, he was reluctant to part with it so soon. Taking another glance, he noted the date. It was today. Tonight, he was supposed to marry Mary, no wonder half of Lushton and Bridgecrest was at his front door.

He was about to find a pew to sit and stew in, when he heard a voice outside yell, "There's a hole in the wall over there!"

Father Young realized that his church was under siege. It is difficult to find sanctuary in a building without four intact walls. He quickly fled for his quarters, slunk in, and shut the door, just as the first group reached Henry the Pig's personal entrance.

Father Young jammed the door shut with a chair as he heard masses of people filing into the church. It didn't take long before the sounds of brawls could be heard.

"I've sat in that pew for twenty years."

"I don't care how long you sat in it. I'm sitting in it now."

"What makes you think he wants people from Lushton at his wedding? He's *our* priest."

"Mary is from Lushton, you daft fool."

Father Young was aware that his church sounded more like a tavern than a house of God, but he couldn't bring himself to care. As the sounds grew louder, the reality of the situation deepened in his mind. He could see his future life with Mary. He saw himself weeping on day one. As the vision continued, he was celebrating his tenth anniversary still weeping. A heavy pounding on the door pulled him back to the present.

The knocking came from the parsonage back door, and not from the barrier between him and the masses. There was the possibility that it was Mary, but it could also be Mr. Porkshire. So, despite the apparent danger, he cautiously opened the door. It was neither. Bishop Goldheart stood at his threshold.

"I thought you might be back here. Did the page deliver the invite?" the bishop casually said as he walked in.

Father Young nodded, acknowledging that he had.

"I gather that your feelings towards Mary have not improved?"

Father Young shook his head.

"That does make this a sticky situation." Although Bishop Goldheart had tried to come up with a plan on the road, nothing had yet come to mind. "Wasn't there another girl you fancied?" the bishop asked.

"Yes, Fannie," Father Young said emphatically.

Bishop Goldheart was not exactly sure how it would help, but figured she better be present. "Where is she?" he queried.

"I'm really not sure," Father Young answered. "Likely at home."

"Where does she live?"

"In the cottage down the road, in the small valley."

"That muddy area?" Bishop Goldheart questioned in surprise.

"Yes, they raise pigs."

"Oh, right."

"Mr. Porkshire, her father, said he would handle it," said Father Young, hoping that somehow that would be helpful.

"Handle what?" asked Bishop Goldheart.

Father Young shrugged his shoulders. Father Young realized that Mr. Porkshire did not know of the wedding, so that could not have been it. However, Mr. Porkshire had only said he would handle "it" and he said it in such a way that he expected Father Young to know what "it" was. Father Young hoped that if he said "it" in the same way that Bishop Goldheart might somehow know what "it" was. But clearly, this had not worked.

"I think I better go and fetch her and her father. The good news is that nobles have begun to arrive with their carriages, and they clearly did not plan for the small size of this church so they should be backed up for some time trying to get in. Stay here and try not to get married," he gave as a final caution, then he walked out the door.

Again, Father Young sat waiting. Bishop Goldheart had been correct. Soon a line of carriages stretched out of sight down the lane in front of the small church. Father Young could hear the nobles yelling at the coachmen to proceed, to which the coachmen calmly informed their nobles that the coach was unable to transport itself through solid objects such as the coach in front of them. Some of the less high-minded nobles had resorted to walking, but most, refusing to be seen in muddy boots at a wedding, simply sat.

Inside the chapel, henchmen and coachmen tried to convince, bribe, or bully peasants to allow room for their particular noble. It was not long before, adding to the ruckus, Father heard a knock on the door, the lone barrier betwixt him and a dark future. Father Young looked much as one might if he knew the Grim Reaper was coming for lunch. The knocks became more frequent and louder until the person on the other side gave up on this approach and tried to push the door ajar. Luckily, Father Young liked good sturdy chairs and the one he employed as gatekeeper was equal to the task. Finally, the knocker spoke in a high-pitched voice that attempted to ring out above the chaos, "This is Duke Diddlehop and I demand that you open this door!"

Father Young had no desire to move, but when a duke demands you act, you act. In a rather quick motion, he stood up, moved the chair, and before he could half open the door, the well-dressed duke came falling through it and onto the floor. Father Young quickly helped him up. "What . . . is the meaning of this?" yelled the duke as he stood.

"Sorry, your grace," Father Young stuttered, "I had closed the door to . . . prepare myself."

"Well, you have done a terrible job of it," said the duke as he looked over Father Young. "You don't look at all ready for the wedding. The church is full of peasants. I didn't invite any peasants. There are horrid accommodations for our carriages, and your outfit . . . it's awful."

With each new complaint, Father Young got out, "Sorry, your grace."

"Also, this church of yours is horribly small."

Father Young would have said sorry again but thought of no way he would have been able to enlarge the church with a half-day's notice.

"Also, my good man, I am not sure you are aware, but there is a rather large hole on the one side."

"Yes, your grace, I had noted it."

"Well, I would fix that if I were you," the duke said matter-of-factly. "Where is that bloomin' bishop?" asked the duke.

Father Young should've thought to lie and pretend not to know, but he was so anxious to keep the duke's blood pressure down that he quickly said, "He has gone to fetch Mr. Porkshire, your grace."

"Who is Mr. Porkshire?"

"Local pig farmer, your grace."

"Local pig farmer!" the duke repeated in outrage. "He had better be here soon. I guess we have some time. My Aunt Penelope has refused to walk, and I doubt we can get her carriage any closer. I've sent four men to carry her, but knowing Auntie, I had better send four more. They may take some time, so you, my dear priest, have ten minutes to change into something more suitable. Then you had better be in front of the altar waiting for your bride." The duke left, slamming the door behind him. Father Young's wardrobe hadn't entered his mind, but he saw the duke's point. He probably shouldn't marry in the brown monk's habit he currently wore. Unfortunately, the only other outfit he had were the robes he wore for Mass. He changed, and as he did, he hoped and fervently prayed that Bishop Goldheart would soon be knocking on the back door. But even after Father Young was fully changed, the door remained silent.

As instructed by the duke, in exactly ten minutes, he opened the door and entered the church. Before him was a strange amalgam of society. Duchesses sat trying to get servants to push peasants back. But for each one that was removed, another poured in, being pushed by the throng behind them. Every seat was full, and bricks fell from the side of the hole as more people tried to push in for a view.

Diddlehop was yelling at groups of peasants, demanding that they leave. They insisted that they were trying but couldn't get out through the throng. Mary stood in front of the altar delighted to be at the center of the chaos.

It took a moment for them to notice, but once Father Young was seen, the room began to quiet. Noticing the change, Duke Diddlehop turned, and giving up on the peasants, he said, "Oh good, Father." Then looking him over as he approached, "You look . . . better, not good, but better. So where is Bishop Goldheart?"

From outside the break in the wall came a voice, "I'm back here, your grace."

Father Young could clearly hear that it was Bishop Goldheart and felt both relieved and afraid. Why had he not come back to his quarters?

The duke yelled out, "I will have the head of any peasant who does not let the bishop through!" Henry VIII had a wife for every time the duke used this threat, yet it was still effective, and quickly a part in the crowd appeared.

Through the opening came Bishop Goldheart dragging someone reluctantly by the ear. Whomever it was pulled back, almost as hard as Bishop Goldheart pulled them forward. But the sober bishop's grip was well in place as he thrust the man into the opening near the altar.

It was John the mason who stood like a deer in the torch lights as he looked up at Mary. "Mary?"

"John?" she smiled and giggled.

"Who is this?" demanded the duke.

John and Mary ignored them as they both stared into each other's eyes.

"The groom," Bishop Goldheart said matter-of-factly. He turned to the crowd before the duke could voice his displeasure, and said, "Ladies and gentlemen, dukes, duchesses, earls, and barons, you have come to witness Father Young marry Mary of Lushton." Mary let out a verbal cooing at the mention of her name. The bishop ignored the outburst and continued, "And you shall see Father Young marry Mary." The relief on the duke's face was obvious until Bishop Goldheart continued, "You shall see Father Young marry Mary of Lushton to John, the mason."

The church instantly exploded in uproar. Mary's mother fainted as Mary and John embraced. Nobles were yelling at the duke, some stood to leave as a gesture of their disapproval. It was only a gesture, as there was no hope of getting through the crowd. The duke turned a strange shade of red. The bishop had played his cards well. Had he come to the duke separately, then the duke would have forced the priest to marry Mary. But it would be difficult to turn it around now. Bishop Goldheart had pushed a boulder off the cliff, and it was not coming back.

Father Young felt like the boulder had not fallen off the cliff but rather off his back. He had never felt so free. But as with so many instances in life, with that freedom came some sorrow. Sorrow for his savior, Bishop Goldheart, who now stood before him. Given the look on the duke's face, Father Young wondered how long the bishop would be able to stand at all. Taking the peasants' heads may have been an idle threat but the duke was now looking longingly at the bishop's. And Father Young understood that Bishop Goldheart had just risked his life to save him from an unhappy marriage.

Bishop Goldheart was aware of the sacrifice he was making. He had done some real soul searching on the way to the Porkshires'. Upon finding them not there, he had headed back to the church. It was on that walk he thought of his life. A lost chance at love had defined his life up to that point. In his mind he saw Father Young becoming a drunk, spending his time at the local pub, bemoaning his marriage, and how Fannie had gotten away. It was this vision of the father, the young priest he had grown to care for, that had made up the bishop's mind; he would act no matter the cost.

And despite the fact that he was sure he would likely pay the ultimate price, he too was feeling freer and happier than he ever had. The thought of freeing Father Young made the bishop smile from ear to ear, even if death was around the next corner. He quickly realized that he enjoyed this moment even more when he turned away from the reddish blob of fury that was the duke's head and looked over the chaos of the crowd.

Looking out, he noticed a peasant dodge the cane of a local baron. As the peasant bobbed, missing the brunt of the blow, the bishop thought he noticed someone just behind them. This was not just any face, but her face, and suddenly, his next step was clear. After all, *why not*, he thought. He was already a dead man.

No one could silence the crowd except the man who had started the uproar. After all, he had brought some pretty exciting stuff to the table so far. So as soon as he yelled out, "And that is not all!", instantly silence fell. The only sounds that could be heard were Edwina's squeals outside.

"Is Miss Elizabeth Denine here?"

The bishop's tendency to pull forward random peasants who ruined his day, was getting on the duke's nerves. The whole point of this exercise was to get his family out of scandal. He had found a scandal that would make people forget about his sister. Unfortunately, it was about a duke inviting nobles to a tiny church to see a peasant's wedding. Another peasant from the crowd could only make this worse.

"Wait, Bishop," fumed the duke. "What does this common peasant have to do with anything?"

The bishop again decided it was best to play to the crowd rather than engage the duke one on one.

"Of course, you, your grace, would not invite all of this nobility just for a peasant's wedding."

Now the bishop even had the duke's attention.

"But what if there were to be the wedding of a bishop?"

The duke then completely forgave the bishop his past transgressions. No noble had yet to have a bishop marry. He would be the first and the dramatic way it was being announced would only add to the story. This would speed the tale's travel through the kingdom.

With all the excitement of Henry VIII spotting a new maiden at court, he asked, "So Bishop, are you getting married today?"

The bishop turned to Miss Denine who had made her way to the front. "That, your grace, is up to this, most uncommon of peasant women, to decide. What do you say, Elizabeth? How would you like to save this brash bishop's life in more ways than one?"

Duke Diddlehop was a little taken aback. Proposals in his world were business transactions made by men. He almost jumped in and demanded that she marry the bishop, but for some reason, he did something he had never done before and held his tongue. If only the bishop had still been Catholic, they could have counted this as his first miracle of sainthood.

Miss Denine, for a moment, was also speechless. Each moment she didn't speak only increased her tears. Finally, the crowd began to turn to their neighbors and whisper, "Did she say anything yet?" or "What did she say?"

At some point some ambitious peasant wishing to speed things up just yelled out, "She said yes!"

Long before she had gained any form of composure, it was universally thought she had accepted, and she cared not to correct the error. While the crowd was still coming to grips with just how historic an event they were witnessing, they all began to make obvious statements of fact to their pewmates. "I bet we are going to see a bishop marry!"

While the noise continued, Miss Denine leaned into the only person that needed to hear her say it and she whispered, "Yes, but no free drinks."

His excitement level exceeded the need to verbalize, so he did something he had always hoped to do but never could. He allowed his arms to reach around Miss Denine and embrace her. The rest of the world melted away as they continued their embrace and then he turned and allowed his lips to touch hers. He felt a warmth greater than any drink she'd ever given him. This increased the excitement in the room. The less controllable peasants began to whoop and holler at the sight of their bishop locking lips with Miss Denine. And for his own benefit, the bishop used this as an excuse to extend his kiss.

It took some time for the actual ceremonies to begin. The first, the peasant wedding as it was recorded in the history books of Mary and John the mason, went off fairly straightforward except for the constant loud sobs made by Mary's mother.

The audience sat restlessly tolerating the first ceremony much like the opening knights at a joust. You came for the main event but put up with squires and knights-in-training maiming each other, even if it wasn't that exciting, knowing that the real action was to come.

By the time the first ceremony ended, it was well past nightfall and torches were lit to allow people to see. The night was perfect. It was warm for Bridgecrest, and the sky was cloudless, allowing a full moon to shine in through the broken wall.

Both Bishop Goldheart and Miss Denine's clothes were more appropriate for a day's worth of walking than for a wedding, but both were old enough to know each other's beauty could not be seen by those in attendance no matter how ornately they had been dressed.

Once Bishop Goldheart's ceremony started, the audience was no longer merely tolerant but realized this was the main event. Therefore, they sat in perfect attention, trying to soak up each moment almost as much as Miss Denine and the bishop did. Father Young never enjoyed performing a ceremony so much. When he finally said, "In the name of The Father, Son and Holy Spirit," the whooping and hollering began again. Bishop Goldheart, remembering back to his days as the peasant's priest, grabbed Miss Denine and dipped her in a passionate kiss. None would admit it, but even a few of the nobles got lost in the moment. The Baroness of Canterbury even threw a hat in the air, hitting the Earl of Sussex. Although some later claimed that this had more to do with the earl's recent visit and the fact that some silver had gone missing than her overexuberance, but we may never know.

Eventually, people realized that there wasn't anything exciting left to see and started to file out. Peasants and nobles alike now realized how late it was and how tired they were.

Before long the only occupants of the once sardine-like filled church were the bishop, his bride, Father Young, and the Porkshires. After the standard congratulations were handed out, Father Young had to ask, "How did you convince John to marry Mary?"

"Well, I first went to go get the Porkshires, but no one was there," Bishop Goldheart replied.

"That would be my fault," interrupted Mr. Porkshire. "See Fannie and I were discussing some things yesterday." As he said this, Fannie smiled at Father Young in a way that made him feel far more awake than he'd ever felt at this late hour. "And Fannie wanted to discuss some things with her aunt, so we weren't there because we were on our way to Lushton. Fortunately, Elizabeth caught us on the road. Bishop, I would never have headed to Lushton if I had known all this was going on."

"No need to apologize," said the bishop. "It only worked out because you weren't there. See, after you were found missing, I decided I had to act. Then I remembered a youth coming into confession last week. He told me he needed to confess to hitting a priest. Of course, I knew he was one of the . . ." He almost said "swine" but remembered whose company he was in. " . . . ruffians who had beat up on you, Father. As part of his confession, he gave the names of his accomplices." As the bishop spoke, Father Young realized he had never told anyone who his assailants were.

"At the top of the list was John. On my way to the church, I figured my best chance of saving Father Young was finding a substitute. I went straight into the crowd, and the Lord did provide, I found John and gave him a simple choice. Either rot in jail for assaulting a man of the cloth or marry the beautiful Mary. I thought he would be conflicted, but he was all excited to marry Mary. Turns out he used to be in love with her and had been run off by her mother. The only reason I had to drag him out of the crowd by the ear was that he demanded going somewhere to clean up before he married her, something I knew there wasn't time for. So, I pulled him out of the crowd and announced my plan."

"When did I become part of your plan?" asked Mrs. Denine-Goldheart.

The bishop smiled, "I wish I could say ten years ago, but it wasn't until I saw your face in the audience." They smiled and snuggled into each other the way newlyweds do and in such a way as to leave everyone else in the room thinking this was somewhere betwixt cute and painfully uncomfortable.

Bishop Goldheart sensed that the others were tipping towards discomfort and with a desire to not make it even more uncomfortable said, "Well, I think Mrs. Goldheart and myself should go see if there's a room in the inn." Everyone understood and they left.

With one group leaving, the conversation kind of died. Mr. Porkshire was the first to speak, "Me and the Missus better be getting back to the homestead." Mrs. Porkshire clearly did not want to leave and would rather stick around while Father Young and Fannie worked things out, but she could see that the votes were three to one, so she got up and took Mr. Porkshire's arm and headed out.

Then there were two. Fannie walked over to the front pew and sat. Father Young followed and sat, leaving more than enough room for a third person between them. For a time, silence ruled as Father Young debated what, if anything, to say. The two were comfortable with silence. After a minute, Fannie rose. Of course, this made Father Young rise as well. She walked over and sat down next to where he had been sitting. He looked down, smiled, and then sat by her side. Again, silence continued. Father Young thought that what had kept him from speaking was his fear of knowing if Fannie returned his affections, but now her feelings seemed clear, yet he was still as unsure what to say as before.

As he sat, he saw her offer her hand, which he gently reached out and held. It was somewhat shocking to Father Young how much simply touching her skin caused such a rise in his heart rate and emotions.

He looked at her and she gave him a simple smile, he smiled in return. She rose and guided him hand in hand to the open wall.

Below the crude arch they stood. Father Young had never realized how beautiful the view was outside his little church. The fields outside, with its dew-covered grass, glittered in the moonlight. He followed the moonlight over the field and then to Fannie and looked into her brown eyes. Her smile had not changed, and she continued to look up at Father Young.

"When did you decide you loved me?" she asked in such a wonderfully simple way.

Father Young had been so worried about talking to her that he was amazed how the silence had calmed him. For some reason, he now felt very natural. He said, "Since I saw you walk into this church. The day your family came to town." She leaned her head against his shoulder.

"Why didn't you ever talk to me when you were over talking to Pa?" she asked.

"Priests are not the best at talking to women," was his simple and honest reply.

She leaned into him. "You know, I'm glad John knocked you out."

"Why?" Father Young asked gently, not wanting her to move her head.

"How else would I have gotten to know you, and love you?"

If a girl sits next to you, holds your hand, and lays her head on your chest, there is a good chance she likes you. But hearing those words vocalized is comforting and equal or more important than all the outward signs.

Silence again overtook them but not due to there being too little to say. Rather, no words seemed good enough for the moment. Both were content to finally be enjoying each other's company. Suddenly a question occurred to Father Young, "So when are we going to get married?" Father Young asked. To him it seemed a perfectly rational question.

But the question was not the right one from Fannie's point of view. Father Young knew it because her head rose and she said, "Are we getting married?"

Father Young quickly went into damage control. He'd thought he was done, over, victory won, dragon slain. So, he astutely said, "Um."

Fannie realized he didn't understand and came to his rescue.

"I have never been asked."

Father Young felt better instantly. He knew exactly what to do. Getting down on one knee, he looked up into her face and said, "Fannie Porkshire, will you marry me?"

She bent forward, bringing her face close to his, looked him in the eye, and said, "Of course, I will."

They kissed in the soft moonlight as Edwina ran by, knocking a few more bricks onto the floor.

In Closing

This is the portion of the story where I say, "And they lived happily ever after." But I feel it is incumbent on myself to give more detail and admit to the reader why and how I know so much about what transpired in Bridgecrest and Lushton around 1558.

I myself was raised in Stratford, not far from the town of Lushton, and I often heard my father and others speak of Bishop Goldheart. Why the interest in this story? Is it not natural that a son wonders how he came to be? How his parents ever met and came to bring him into the world? Such was my curiosity. And as I began my life as a writer, I was determined to make it the first story I ever told. I was able to spend weeks between Lushton and Bridgecrest interviewing the people who grace the pages of this tale. Henry and Edward still spend their days debating the ins and outs of English politics.

Bishop Goldheart would remain in Lushton, where he became a legend. They had to expand the Cathedral twice to accommodate the crowds who came to Mass each Sunday, but his real service was done Monday-Saturday. He was still a regular at Miss Denine's or should I say Mrs. Goldheart's establishment. She continued to serve the people of Lushton drinks, that is except for Bishop Goldheart, who completely gave up drinking, at least in its alcoholic form. In fact, the one sin that he was guilty of was refusing to follow the church's stance on wine for communion, regularly sneaking in grape juice. But his lack of indulgence didn't keep him from the tavern. He went to truly serve any way he could. If there was a traveler stranded, the bishop helped them find a way home. If there was a man drinking off a fight with his spouse, the bishop was there to counsel or console, whichever was needed. When he died, England mourned the loss more than if they had lost the queen.

Mr. and Mrs. Porkshire would enjoy their days in the mud hollow in Bridgecrest. He continued to improve his pig farming technique, and as it improved, so did his profits. By the time he and the Missus died, the field of mud also held a home that dwarfed the cathedral in Lushton.

Father Young and Fannie never did find any love for pig farming. In their case, the pig-loving gene skipped a generation. Their oldest son Clarence loved pigs in a way that made his grandfather happier than the first day he found himself nose-to-snout with a pig. Clarence would marry into a title and inherit the home and the pigs, becoming the first Earl of Emsworth.

Fannie and Father Young would end up having four children. Fannie stayed home raising the children until they all had homes of their own and then convinced her husband to take his ministry on the road. They retired and spent their days traveling around Europe.

And as for my father and mother. Oh? Did you think I was Father Young's son? I can see how that mistake could be made. No, I am the son of John and Mary. Don't be too harsh in how I portray them. They both reviewed the manuscript recently and said, "You were too kind to us. We were fools in every way imaginable in those days. Thank goodness Bishop Goldheart pulled us out of the crowd and stuck us together. Who knows what would become of us if that hadn't happened?"

And truly I don't know, but what I do know is my father realized quickly that masonry was not for him, but somehow on his way back to Lushton, he and Peter, the messenger, who had considered him so unneighborly, struck up a conversation. They decided that if people would pay to send messages, then surely, they would pay you to transport and trade goods. They began a very successful business as merchants.

Of course, I am convinced time will prove that their greatest accomplishment was me. After all, if this story doesn't make me famous, I am confident that some of my writing will. For my next work, perhaps moving from bishops and priests to princes and kings? Whatever I write I plan to be a credit to the Shakespeare name.

Sincerely, your humble servant
William.

A Note to the Reader

First of all, I want to thank you for reading *Of Pigs and Priests*. I love to write, but it is immensely more rewarding to write and be read than simply to write. My purpose in writing to you at the conclusion of my book is twofold. One to give you a little more detail on the inspiration for the book and then to ask you a favor.

Of Pigs and Priests is the first book I ever completed, even though it was published after my first novel, *The Business Proposal*, which is also a must read. (Sorry, shameless plug.) The origins of this book are very easy to place. It was a dream. I was a Catholic priest in the dream. I was there as England transitioned to the Church of England and I was suddenly able to date and marry. At that moment I wondered how very interesting it would be to go from sworn celibate to most eligible bachelor.

I can place the dream fairly closely to the day because it occurred while I was taking a class at University of New Mexico in Las Cruces. It was a two-week course on how to inspect bridges. Hence the town of Bridgecrest. I took the class in February 2012, and it must have been fairly early in the class because I spent every break I got during the class writing the book. (For those of you who drive over one of the many bridges I inspected in the southwestern United States, don't worry, I also paid attention in the class on occasion.)

The fact that my subconscious was thinking about a historical event that occurred in England in the 1500's is a testament to the amazing teaching skills of Ms. Farr, a talented European history teacher that so seared the information into my brain that it was invading my dreams over ten years later.

Whether you call this an historical fiction, I leave up to you. The basic timeline and major events are correct. King Henry VIII really did of course leave the Catholic Church and began the Church of England. The archbishop of Canterbury under King Edward did publish *The Common Book of Prayer* and Article 32 was included, but true to the book, it was not implemented until years later when Queen Elizabeth came to the throne. King Edward, being young as he was, did have a regent, but it was not Duke Diddlehop. Duke John Dudley was his name. Much of what Diddlehop went through is based on Dudley. Like Diddlehop, Dudley abjured the protestant faith, but unlike Diddlehop, it did not save his life. He was executed under Mary in 1553. His brother Andrew, who was also condemned to death, did find a way to live on until 1559, so consider Diddlehop a mix of the brothers.

It was partially this change in his survival status, and the fact that I thought Diddlehop was a funny name, that convinced me to deviate from history in this respect. Another important truth or line up in time is that John and Mary Shakespeare were indeed married in 1557 or 58; historians debate on the exact timing. It was this timing that made me determined to include their dear son William.

But everything else, the towns, the people, and the story is all a figment of my own imagination. Historians will also argue that I got many things wrong, and they would be correct. A good example is the term Anglicans. The term Anglican does indeed go back into the 1500's but it was not generally used as the name for members of the faith until well into the 19th century. So why did I call them Anglicans in the book? The idea of Henry making his sign calling him and his fellow parishioners Angel Cans was too good to give up, so I left it, despite its historical inaccuracy.

But another point that historians and others may take exception to is my light treatment of what is seen as a dark and oppressive time. In this I take exception to their exception, and it became one of the main reasons why I wrote the book. I am not blind to the economic and political struggles that existed in 16th century England, but the idea that they were not a jovial and happy people, I think is in error.

Our world is filled with many people who are economically disadvantaged. People who lack basic necessities of water to drink and food to eat, yet despite these amazing challenges, among the most impoverished of people, I see happiness. If there is one thing the amazing comparative wealth between nations in our world can teach us, it is that happiness and positivity are not monopolized by the wealthy. They may have more food, more technology, nicer clothes, faster cars, and bigger homes, but they don't necessarily have more happiness or laughter. This has led me to believe that those in the 1500's smiled and laughed much more than we give them credit for. If my book helps portray this, then I think it might be more accurate than many history books that cover the time period.

The last thing I want to ask of you, dear reader, is a favor. It is amazingly difficult for a new author to get "discovered." I feel exceptionally honored that I have been able to be published and that you found me. But if you liked this book, the only chance I have to be found by others depends on readers like you. Please consider leaving me a review on Amazon, Goodreads, or some other platform. A personal post on any social media would also greatly help, or even better, talk to a friend about the book.

And if you want to hear about when my next book comes out or what else I am working on, sign up for my newsletter through my webpage nathanielkgee.com. If you want to really make my day, feel free to reach out to me and let me know that you enjoyed the book. I can be reached on my email gee.nathaniel@gmail.com, through @authornathanielgee on Instagram or nathanielgee on Facebook.

Again, thanks so much for reading, and I can't wait to meet you in the next book.

About the Author

The only thing Nathaniel Gee loves more than writing is support-ing his wife and eight children, which is why he works as a Dam Safety Engineer. His determination to become a writer came from an inspirational school counselor who said that he would be a much better engineer than a writer. He was a well-loved writer of his local newspaper and continues writing on his blog at www.thegeebrothers.com, professional journals in Dam Safety, and in his favorite genres—romantic comedy and detective fiction. He also has a YouTube chan-nel, Geelightful, where his children are far more popular than he is. You can reach out to Nathaniel or check out what else he is up to at nathanielkgee.com.

Scan to visit

nathanielkgee.com